SECRET OF THE LOCKED TRUNK

DEDICATION

For my parents,
Robert and Doris Holm,
who taught me that I
could do all things through Christ
who is our strength.

SECRET OF THE LOCKED TRUNK

JANET HOLM MCHENRY

2699

ChariotVICTOR
PUBLISHING
A DIVISION OF COOK COMMUNICATIONS

ANNIE SHEPARD MYSTERIES
Mystery at the Fairgrounds
Secret of the Locked Trunk
Mystery at the Old Stamp Mill

Designer: Andrea Boven
Cover Illustration: Rick Johnson

CIP information available upon request.

1 2 3 4 5 6 7 8 9 10   01 00 99 98 97

Chariot Books is an imprint of ChariotVictor Publishing,
a division of Cook Communications, Colorado Springs, Colorado 80918
Cook Communications, Paris, Ontario
Kingsway Communications, Eastbourne, England

CONTENTS

1

THE ORANGE

Ahhhhhh!

A woman's scream pierced the foggy darkness.

I stopped dead in my tracks and grabbed my two new friends by their arms. "Will you guys quit singing that crazy country song? This could be serious. Or dangerous."

My two friends were singing and swinging each other around by the elbows. They were not in the mood to take me seriously. Scream or no scream.

We were running down a road that wound around behind the county fairgrounds past two quiet homes and then dead ended at my house, which was on the edge of the national forest.

"Just because someone's screaming doesn't mean it's another case for the After School Sleuths," laughed Maria.

"Well, whatever it is, it's just around that bend," I said. "Let's go."

And then we heard it again. "Ahhhhhhh!!!" Kind of bloodcurdling. Or at least hair-curling.

"I, uh, think I'll just, uh, stay right behind this bush here and scout things out while you two go on ahead." That was Alia, and she wasn't laughing now. The third member of the After School Sleuths, Alia was petite, blonde and fair, and she was the timid one. Usually, anyway. But sometimes she came on strong at just the right moment. This obviously wasn't the right moment.

"Oh, no you don't, skinny ninny. You're coming with us." That was Maria. She was the outgoing one. She had gorgeous dark hair in a thick French braid and dark eyes and a build that all the other eighth grade girls at Mountain Center Middle School envied, but she could probably outwrestle a cougar.

On the other hand, you could describe me as ordinary. Medium length, medium brown hair. Average complexion, average nose, average blue eyes. I'm almost ordinary everything, except that I'm five foot, eight inches tall. In the eighth grade, that is NOT average—that is embarrassing, since I hover over all the boys. And I don't hover very well, either. Mom says *Anne* means *graceful*, but that's pretty funny since I flunked out of ballet after half a lesson.

"C'mon," I said, rubbing my cold hands on the sleeves of my extra large Dodger blue, hooded sweatshirt, which hung way down over my jeans. "After all, what's the worst thing that could happen?" That's what my dad always says. Actually, I wasn't as sure as I sounded after that last scream.

"We could get kidnapped," said Alia, looking around

nervously. "Or mugged. Or...ahhhhhhh!!! Look out!"

Out of the cold mist streaked a man in a nylon black jogging suit with a hood pulled over his head. We jumped to the right side of the scarcely two-lane dirt road as he sprinted by without a pause or a sound except his rhythmic breathing. In a moment he was gone into the fog behind us.

"That's it. I'm going home," whispered Alia.

"Alone? In this fog?" asked Maria.

Alia grumbled and followed us slowly.

Just ahead, near the intersection with Fairgrounds Road we saw something orange. Actually, it was someone orange. A woman was leaning over a bicycle. "Yoohoo, hello! Yoohoo, hello!" She was waving at us. As if we could miss her. She was a ball of neon orange. Neon orange field jacket. Neon orange stretch pants. And a neon orange knit hat. The only thing she was wearing that wasn't neon orange was her pair of very round, white eyeglasses. In fact, she looked like a neon orange—fruit, I mean. That's how round she was.

"Oh, my goodness gracious, are you angels of mercy or what?"

We all gathered around her bike. The front tire was completely flat.

She took a dramatic pose with her arms outstretched. It was then that I noticed she was carrying a briefcase on her back, like someone would carry a backpack. "There I was being chased by the hooded jogger in the fog. I pedaled faster and faster. He ran faster and faster. I turned. He turned. So I screamed."

"We, uh, heard you, ma'am," I said. "Are you..."

She ignored me. "And then I remembered. I'm near the Shepard house. I sold that house to them this summer. They seemed like nice people. So I zipped around the corner of the fairgrounds and turned onto Fairgrounds Road. And he zipped around the corner and turned onto Fairgrounds Alley. And then... And then..."

"And then?" gulped Alia, her gold-rimmed glasses slipped on her nose as her eyes widened.

"I got a flat," the woman said. "And I screamed again."

"And the man?" I asked.

"He's gone. That's the good news. The bad news is that I'm stranded," she grimaced.

The woman took a quick breath and grabbed my hand to shake it. "Hey, I'm Esther Reel. Reel Real Estate. I bicycle around a lot. It's the easiest way to get around to all the nooks and crannies to find out what houses are for sale. If I can get a listing, it could mean next month's bills are paid. Hey, aren't you Annie Shepard?"

I nodded.

"So you heard me scream?"

Maria laughed. "Mrs. Reel, I think everyone on this side of the Sierra Nevada heard you scream. Are you okay?"

"I'm fine. Just a little shook up by that jogger. Hey, can I use your phone? I'll call my neighbor and see if he'll come pick up my cycle and me."

"No problem," I said. "In fact, my brother, Link, could probably give you a ride."

We walked back up the slight grade to my house. I wasn't as worried as a few minutes before, since I figured anything, man or beast, would probably be repelled by the neon orange walking stoutly in front of us. Probably, I figured, the jogger was just using her as a guide in the dark.

I could see our front porch light through the fog. A large covered porch hugged the front of the house, which stood two and a half stories tall. Scalloped trim followed the pointy roof lines. The old Victorian, surrounded by wide yards and tall pines, could have looked mysterious, but warm lights beckoned from each window. I was kind of getting used to living in Mountain Center. We had moved from L.A. a few months before. My parents left their law firm for a feed store business. I left shopping centers, Disneyland, and the beach for a town with one stoplight and pine trees. But it was growing on me. I'd made two friends—Maria and Alia—and we'd started our own sleuth business, the After School Sleuths. We'd already solved one case and thought we'd found another. But it just seemed that all Esther needed was a ride home.

I opened the gate to the white picket fence. The lights from the porch were seemingly burning the fog away from our house. And then I noticed him. The man in the hooded jogging suit was at my front door talking with my mom.

2

HIDDEN STAIRCASE

"That's *him!*" whispered Esther, hiding behind us. "The hooded jogger."

The man continued to talk with my mom, who stayed behind the screen door of the house. He wore a shiny black nylon jogging suit with a large hood that completely covered his head and face.

"What is he doing here?" asked Alia, shivering. She shouldn't have been cold in her blue and white Mountain Middle School Grizzlies sweatshirt and matching pants; but she pulled the hood over her French braided hair and the sleeves over her hands. Maria was dressed exactly the same, but her sweatshirt was tied around her waist. She was hot. Alia was cold. Maria was dark-skinned. Alia was pale. Maria was enthusiastic and daring. Alia was shy and timid. They were totally different, yet exactly alike. I was somewhere in the middle.

"Only one way to find out," I whispered back, heading up the stairs. "Follow me."

But as we climbed the half dozen wooden stairs up to the covered front porch of the old house, the jogger said, "Well, thanks anyway," turned away from us and jogged down the stairs and back into the fog.

"Mom, who..."

"Annie, who..."

Mom and I interrupted each other.

"Oh, Mom, you remember Mrs. Reel who sold us the house?" I waved toward the neon orange.

"Oh, yes, hello, Mrs. Reel," Mom said. "Esther, isn't it?"

Short, petite mom, who used to wear power suits, now stood two inches taller in boots, jeans, and a black T-shirt with rolled up sleeves that read, "Reno Rodeo." Lightly freckled, her face wore signs of a long day but her ever-perky bobbed hair still hung perfectly.

"Yes, Mrs. Shepard," said Esther. "But to echo your daughter here, who was..." She waved toward the fog.

"Oh, some local antique dealer. He was jogging in the neighborhood and just stopped to see if we had any antiques for sale. He wondered if any had been left with the house when we bought it."

"How odd," said Esther. "I don't recall anything left in the house. And you haven't found anything hidden in a closet...like a trunk, perhaps?"

Mom shook her head. "That's odd, Mrs. Reel," Mom said. "He asked about a trunk too."

Mom stared at Mrs. Reel quizzically. So did I. Was the neon orange on a fishing expedition too? It certainly seemed so.

I interrupted. "Mom, Mrs. Reel needs a ride. She got a flat

tire down the road on her bicycle."

Mom nodded and called for Link. He had a new old pick-up truck that he was proud to use for any errand. Soon the two were off and Maria, Alia, and I headed up to my room.

My room fit my usual mood: blue. My bedspread, throw rugs, pillows, and beanbag blended into a roomful of blue-ness. It was a great escape...sometimes literally, with a door that led to a small balcony over the front porch.

There we flopped down on the dozen throw pillows on my otherwise wooden floor, gazing up at the ceiling and try-ing to make sense of the weird goings-on.

"Why would they both mention a trunk?" asked Maria.

"I don't know," I said. "But my whole room is a whole lot of old junk. Hand-me-downs from relatives I never met. That antique dealer could take the whole mess, and I wouldn't miss it.

"And this old house. There's always something to do—chop firewood, paint fences, caulk the windows. My parents are driving me nuts lately. I never had to do this stuff in L.A.—we could always pay someone to do it. But now I'm the hired hand around here. Except there's no 'hired' part about it. I should call it slave labor. I mean, I can't figure what's up with my parents lately."

"What's up..." asked Alia.

"Right," I said, "what's up?"

"No, said Alia, pointing to the ceiling. "I mean, what *is* up...there?"

She was right. Dangling just a couple inches from the ceil-ing was a rope with a wooden crosspiece at its end.

"I don't know," I said. "Let's check it out."

I grabbed the old wooden chair at my old desk and

dragged it across the room until it was under the rope. On my tiptoes, I could barely reach the handle, which was hanging about six inches from the ceiling. I pulled but nothing happened. I pulled again, putting my whole weight underneath, when all of a sudden, the whole ceiling seemed to give way and come down toward me. I jumped for the floor, closing my eyes and putting my hands over my head, not sure of what had happened.

When nothing fell on me or hit me on the head, I opened my eyes. Maria and Alia were standing next to me, speechless, with their mouths open. Just inches before us a staircase had dropped about halfway down into the room. It led up into a dark room above us.

Maria peered up into the black hole. "It looks like it's a pretty large room. Want to try it? Look, the staircase folds all the way down." She unfolded the bottom half of the staircase until it reached the floor of my room right next to my bed.

Alia looked nervously up the staircase. "Maybe we should tell your parents."

I looked toward the open door of my room. "No," I said. "This is my room, and this is our secret. Okay?" I looked at Maria and Alia and smiled. I closed my door softly.

They smiled back. "Okay!" both said at once.

I reached for the flashlight on my bedside table near the bottom of the staircase. "Follow me!"

Slowly, I ascended the stairway, pointing the flashlight ahead of me. Maria and Alia were right at my heels. In a few moments we were standing in the center of a small attic room.

"Hey," said Maria, "it's small."

It was disappointingly small. The sides were steeply

slanted so that standing space was limited. Light from the one small round window at the front of the room cast an eerie glow in the musty, dusty place. I scanned the room with the flashlight. In the back corner were several boxes of books.

I walked over and picked up a book.

"What's it say?" asked Maria.

"Mining Method...Mining Method-o-lo-gy," I read. "Just some dumb old stuff."

"Let's get out of here," said Alia. "This place gives me the creeps."

"Okay, just a minute." I moved the flashlight one more time around the room, slowly scanning under the slanted eaves into the dark corners.

"Hey," said Maria. "Do that again. There's something there in that corner."

Squatting down so I could see better, I poked the light into the dark corner. Way under, almost hidden in the darkness, were three shapes.

"Alia," I said. "You're little. Try and squeeze in there and grab whatever those things are." I coaxed her with a little shove.

"Are you nuts? Are you crazy? There could be spiders...or bats...or yuck, dust bunnies in there! No way! You're the ringleader. You do it!" Alia grabbed my flashlight and gave me a little shove.

I gulped and got down on my hands and knees, crawling through the dust until I reached the first item. My own shadow kept me from seeing very well, but I pulled the thing back into the open part of the room.

"It's a cradle," said Maria. "A baby cradle."

Sure enough, it was. It looked like something someone

had made—simple wooden slats joined to a single board bottom with rockers.

I crawled back into the space and pulled out the next object. It was a rocking chair, similarly made with flat slats for the back and rockers, but no arm rests.

"We have one like this," Alia said. "Mom calls it a sewing rocker."

"Annie, this is cool," said Maria. "Go see what that last thing is."

I crawled back one more time, feeling my way across the floor back into the dark corner. I reached the object. It was bigger and boxier.

"Hey," I said, "roll me that flashlight, so I can see what I'm doing."

"Annie," said Alia, "if we roll you the flashlight so you can see what you're doing, we won't be able to see what *we're* doing."

I sneezed. The dust was getting to me. "Alia, at this very moment, what I am doing is more important than what you are doing, which is nothing. Roll me that flashlight!"

After Alia's short moment of whimpering, the flashlight rolled to me. I grabbed it and shone it ahead of me into the corner.

"Eeehhhhh!" I cried.

"What is it?" Alia cried back from the dark.

"A mouse?" cried Maria. "A bat? A spider?"

"No!" I screamed back. "It's a trunk!"

3

CRASH!

"A trunk?" said Alia. "I thought you'd found a dead body or something the way you screamed."

And then for a long moment we were all quiet. What was it with trunks?

I broke the silence. "This is too weird. I feel as though someone is watching us."

"Doo-doo doo-doo, doo-doo doo-doo," sang Maria and Alia mysteriously.

I shined the light on them. The *Twilight Zone* theme song was *not* country. Thank goodness. But they were right. It was an odd coincidence.

I tugged on the trunk. It gave an inch. "Instead of singing, would you please help me? This thing is heavy."

Maria and Alia crouched down. Each of them latched onto one of the two leather belts that secured the trunk and helped me pull on it. Once we had it at the center of the room, we could stand again and look at it. I shined the light over it. It was about two feet by three feet and about two feet tall. Dark brown wooden strips covered wooden and rusted metal sides. Besides the leather straps, it was secured with two latches and a lock in the middle. I tugged on the lock. It would definitely take a key to open it.

"Let's take this stuff downstairs."

"Your folks will find out about the attic," said Maria. "I mean, they'll want to know where this stuff came from."

"True. But I think they'll let me keep it. After all, I found it. I don't care much about the cradle or the rocking chair. But this trunk is kind of interesting. Maybe there's something valuable in it."

Maria's and Alia's eyes bugged out.

"Sure," said Maria. "Think about it. Why would two people ask about a trunk? Who cares about trunks? They're pretty ordinary things, aren't they? Weren't they the olden-time suitcases?"

"Yeah," said Alia. "I bet there's a reason that this trunk was stuck way up there in the attic. Maybe someone was hiding something..."

Alia gasped. "...or some *body* in it."

"Alia!" Maria and I both said.

"Gross," I said.

"Yeah," said Maria. "Will you get off the dead body thing?"

"Well, you can just go ahead and tease me," said Alia. "But I read in the paper that the police found the bodies of two babies in a trunk in an attic...and it was just over in Loyalville."

"In Loyalville?" I asked. I knew Loyalville was less than an hour away.

"For real?" asked Maria.

"For real," said Alia.

Again, there was a moment of silence. Which is pretty weird any time three teenaged girls are together. Especially twice in just a few minutes. We each inched away from the trunk toward the attic opening.

I cleared my voice. "This is silly, guys. Let's take these things down to my room so we can get a better look at them."

That was easier said than done. The cradle and rocking chair were pretty light, and I handed them down through the opening to Maria, who easily caught and set them in my room. But the trunk was too heavy. We decided that the best course of action was to slide it down the stairway. They would guide it from the bottom sides of the stairway, and I would hold the leather handle strap on the end and slowly walk it down.

That was the theory. But as soon as I eased the trunk over the edge of the floor down on the ladder, I knew I wouldn't be able to hold it. It was too heavy, too bulky, too awkward. If I held on, I knew I'd be going down with it. And Maria and Alia couldn't quite reach it from the floor.

"Oh, no! Look out!" I shut my eyes as the trunk went, ker-thunk, ker-thunk, ker-thunk, and then BAM! right into my antique bedside table, crumpling it into pieces.

I ran down the stairs and stared at the mess that had been the antique table. The one that used to have drop-leaf sides and delicately spindled legs. The one Great-Aunt Maudie had given to my mother. The one my mother was going to throttle me about!

"Hey look, Annie!" Alia was holding my round, blue ceramic lamp. "The lamp's still in one piece."

"Oh good," I said. "My K mart blue light special lamp is in perfect shape and the table my mother loves is now only good for fire starter. My mom is gonna..."

The door opened. "Annie, what is..." Doomsville. It was Mom. "...going on... Eeeeehhhh! My dearest table that my dearest Aunt Maudie gave to me. Oh, Annie, how could..."

"And what is..." Double Doomsville. It was Dad. "...this staircase here?"

My tall dad still looked sort of lawyerish in his wireframed glasses. But now his sandy blonde hair was always a bit rumpled from wearing a baseball cap. He wore jeans, too, beltless, with a neatly tucked-in white T-shirt with a red-checked logo that read, "Purina."

He walked over and peered up into the attic. "How did you find this?" He looked over toward me. I was trying to stand in front of the trunk, but I knew it was a useless effort. "And what is that thing?" He pointed at the trunk.

I stepped out away from it. "It's a trunk, Dad. It was up in the attic. Just let me explain this."

"You'd better explain quickly, young lady." Mom had walked over to the crumpled table and was trying to see if parts would still fit together.

I stood between them. "We were just innocently lying here on my floor, looking up at the ceiling. When all of a sudden I noticed this..."

Alia a-ahemed. I looked at her.

"I mean, Alia here noticed that there was this small rope with a handle sticking out from the ceiling." I smiled. "So you know me, curious ole Anne. If there's a rope with a handle, I've got to pull it. So I did, and this whole staircase unfolded right before our eyes." I smiled again. It seemed to be working. I mean, Mom and Dad weren't screaming or anything.

"So, of course, if there's a staircase, I've got to go up it. So we did. And there's a whole room up there, Mom, Dad, and in the corner of the room, we found this stuff." I pointed to the cradle and rocking chair that were behind Maria and Alia on the other side of the room. Maria and Alia showed off the cradle and the rocking chair on cue as if they were Vanna.

"And you just threw the trunk down the stairs?" asked Mom.

"No, uh, it just sort of fell, Mrs. Shepard," said Maria.

"Yeah," said Alia. "Annie was really trying to be careful, Mrs. Shepard. It was just an unfortunate accident."

There was an awkward silence. I could feel Mom thinking things over. I looked at Maria and Alia and gave them a thanks-guys look.

"Well, it looks like it was an accident. But sometimes, Annie, you're just so careless. You don't think through the consequences. This table was quite precious to me because it's the only thing that I have from your Great-Aunt Maudie."

She looked at the trunk. "Well, I guess you've got yourself a new bedside table. I can't afford to buy one, so you'll have to use this. I'll probably call the antique dealer about the other things. We certainly don't need a cradle or a rocking chair. And we can use the extra money."

She looked at the crumpled table. "Clean up this mess and then say goodbye to your friends. It's been a long day." She stood in thought again and looked over at Dad. "Odd how those two folks both mentioned a trunk tonight, isn't it, Mark? Did I tell you about that?"

The two of them walked out of my room and down the stairs.

Maria and Alia and I looked back and forth at each other and then stared at the trunk.

It was definitely a doo-doo doo-doo, doo-doo doo-doo thing.

4

KEY TO THE PROBLEM

"Maria," said Alia, "let's help Annie clean this up. I called my folks, and they'll be here in a few minutes to get us."

Maria pulled on the leather end handle to lug the trunk away from the table mess. "You know, this is awfully heavy. There must be something in it."

I thought a moment. *How could we open it?*

Alia mumbled something as she continued to pick up table pieces and put them in my trash basket. Maria was stacking the larger pieces.

I walked over to my dresser and rummaged through the shoe box that held my makeup in the top drawer. My nail file! I held it up and smiled.

I kneeled down in front of the trunk, inserting the file into the lock and twisting it around. It wouldn't give. I looked around the room. *What else could I try?*

My closet was ajar. A coat hanger! I grabbed one, held it up, and smiled. "Grandma Rose told me she uses one all the time on her old '57 Chevy when she gets locked out. Just watch."

I squatted down again and stuck the curved end into the lock, twisting it around. It wasn't budging. I kept trying.

Alia mumbled something again—about keys.

"Yeah, yeah, we know," said Maria. "But why would both the antique dealer and Esther Reel know something about a trunk? Do you think there's a mystery about this house? Maybe this is a famous trunk."

"Who would know a thing like that?" asked Alia.

I looked up, continuing to try the hanger in the lock. "Maybe a teacher? Or a librarian?"

"Yeah," said Maria, "they know everything. Or a museum director. We have a museum in town—maybe there's stuff on local history."

"We could check that out," I said. "Shucks. This isn't working, either." I pulled the hanger out of the lock. What else might...? I surveyed the room, thinking.

Alia mumbled something again.

Maybe my scissors would be a good chisel and my shoe a good enough hammer. I reached for the scissors. "Uh, Alia, what was that you've been saying?" I turned toward her.

She turned around from picking up table pieces. "I've been saying I've got a key collection. New ones, old ones. I find them. People give them to me. I've probably got a couple hundred...."

My mouth began to drop.

"That's right," said Maria. "I've seen them. Maybe she's got one that would work on that lock before you ruin it.

My jaw hit bottom. "Too cool," I said. "When can you get it…When can we…."

"I've got church in the morning." Alia brushed off her hands. The cleanup was done. "Do you guys want to go with me?"

"Nah," said Maria. "I go with my family."

"Sure," I said. "Can you bring your keys to church?"

"Sure," said Alia. "We'll pick you up right before nine for Sunday School."

I picked up the wood pile and carried it down to the living room. Maria followed with the waste basket, and Alia followed her, picking up remnants as we dropped them. We unloaded the mess at the living room wood box.

I looked at the shattered mess for a moment. Poor Great-Aunt Maudie. Good thing she couldn't see her drop-leaf table. Drop leaf. An appropriate name, anyway.

Alia's mom honked, and I walked Maria and Alia to the door. I waved goodbye and climbed the stairs back to my room. It was nice of Alia to invite me to church.

Hmm, church. I'd been wanting to go regularly and this was a good chance to get out of the house. Mom and Dad had really been on my case.

A key? Maybe one in Alia's collection would work in the trunk. How many key designs could there be in the world, anyway? Maybe there was something important, something valuable, in the trunk. There *was* only one way to find out: Find the right key.

In my doorway I stared at the trunk, now sitting beside my bed. What could such a plain-looking thing hold? I could hardly wait to find out.

5

ANOTHER TRUNK SEEKER

"Annie, wake up. Annie, wake up."

Ugh. It was morning.

"Annie! You said you were going to church with the Millers. It's eight o'clock—time to get up."

That was the Mother Alarm.

"Okay, Mom. I'm up. I'm up." I rolled over and opened my eyes. "See? I'm up."

"You're not up. You're still in bed. They'll be here in less than an hour. Oh, Annie, every time I see that trunk I'm going to think of Aunt Maudie's table. Why are you so careless with things like that? First you break the balcony, now the table. Why can't you..."

She sighed and walked over to where the table had been and picked up a few splinters. Then she walked over to the door at the other side of my room—the one that led to the little balcony that stood just over the front porch roof. The balcony that I had recently crashed through.

"Money's tight, Annie. This business has really drained us dry in a short time. I'm not sure we'll be able to pay our bills this month. So, I just would appreciate it if you'd take a little care with things. Everything costs money." Mom ran her fingers through her hair.

I slipped out of bed and stood up as she paused in the hall-way doorway. "I'm sorry, Mom, I didn't know. I could get a job or something."

"No, helping out at the feed store is enough." She looked at the rocking chair and cradle in the corner. "But we don't have a place for those things in this house, so I think we will sell them to that antique dealer."

"Sell them? But, Mom, *I* found them. *I* should get to decide what to do with them. Isn't that fair?"

"Fair? It wasn't fair that you broke my table. Sorry, Annie, I've decided. Now get yourself together so you're ready on time."

I sat down again and rubbed my blurry eyes. The one thing that was worse than waking up to the Mother Alarm was getting the Mother Stress. I didn't need it. I mean, why couldn't she say something like, "Oh, dear Anne, you've worked so hard all this week. Why don't you just lie here a few more minutes and wake up gradually"? Why did it have to be the Guilt and Guillotine routine all the time? Mothers!

"Anne! Hurry up and get some breakfast!"

The voice up the stairway was Dad. He was the Sunday morning chef. That meant he put out the cereal bowls and boxes instead of Mom.

I made a mental note to dawdle. I didn't need Round Two from Dad. I'd had a good enough verbal beating.

My tactics worked. Alia's folks soon honked, and I ran down the stairs with a "See ya later" as I flew through the front door.

Alia's dad was turning around their several years old brown van. I ran down the front walk and slid open the side door of the van.

"Hi, Annie!"

I couldn't believe it. All five Millers said it at once and were smiling the same smile. It was like they'd rehearsed it or something. As I looked at them, I instantly turned red. They were all dressed up, and there I was in my jeans, light blue floral T-shirt, and tennies.

I sat beside Alia in the middle seat. Alia's parents were in the front buckets; Alistair, an older sister, and Amy, a younger sister, sat in the back.

"Hi, everybody. Gee, I didn't know you got all dressed up every Sunday. I thought that was just a Christmas and Easter kind of thing."

Mrs. Miller patted my knee. "That's all right, Annie. Most people dress casually. This is just a Miller tradition. We get dressed up and go out for breakfast every Sunday morning."

After reintroductions, we headed off to Mountain Baptist Church, which is two doors from my grandmother's house. Grandma Rose Martoni, my mom's mom, also goes to Mountain Baptist. I knew she'd flip for joy when she saw me there, so I didn't tell her ahead of time.

The whole idea of church hadn't appealed to me much before I moved to Mountain Center. I had thought the whole Christian thing was a set of rules. But when I moved to Mountain Center, things changed. I felt really alone. My family was busy, and I didn't know Maria and Alia very well. In my loneliness I prayed and asked God to be my one true friend. That was just a couple days ago, and I was beginning to learn what that meant.

Because I was new at this, I didn't think God would mind about my jeans and tennies. I figured He was just glad I was there. Grandma Rose was too. She was dressed in her usual rose-flowered outfit ("Rose" is a perfect name for her), and she introduced me to all her friends. I was expecting to meet all of the over seventy set, but it turned out that her "friends" were kids my age. I was surprised that I recognized many of them from school.

Alia took me to the junior high Sunday School class. I figured we'd learn about some Bible person, but instead everyone was listening to rock music. They all brought their favorite tape or CD, and we had to really listen to the words and write them down. Then the teacher—he was a college student named Joe who shook my hand hard enough to give me wrist-lash—talked about what the words meant.

One of my favorites was a hip-hop kind of thing, and we rocked out on it while it played. But as we discussed the words afterwards, I was surprised that the whole song was about a drug dealer.

"That's sick!" I said. "I never knew that's what it said."

Joe smiled. "Yeah, you have to be careful about what you're

listening to. Imagine how God feels when He sees you pouring that stuff into your brain."

"Try my tape next," said Alia. "It's country. I'm sure it's okay."

But as we listened to the first song, we realized that it was about some drunk guy going out on his wife.

"Sick!" I said again. "Alia, you and Maria have got to stop singing that stuff."

She nodded. "Maybe it would be a good idea to listen to the songs before we buy the tape. Most record stores will let us do that."

It was the coolest class I'd ever been to, Sunday or otherwise. In church Alia and I sat with Grandma Rose and her friends near the front. I was a little embarrassed when she introduced me and called me her "little Annie."

The minister talked about how the fear of the Lord was the key to treasure. I'm not sure he was thinking the same kind of treasure that I was, but it sure seemed like another doo-doo doo-doo thing, him talking about keys. He explained that fear wasn't a being scared kind of thing, but a respect and love and worship kind of thing. I could handle that. I mean God is God. You've got to give the guy in charge some respect.

"Did you hear that?" asked Alia after the service. "The key thing?"

"Yes," I said. "I'm beginning to think there may not be coincidences anymore. Just stuff God does."

"Like the trunk?" Alia said.

"Yeah, did you bring the keys?" I asked. "We've got to get

that trunk unlocked. I bet there's some neat stuff inside."

A man next to us turned around. "Excuse me, ladies, were you talking about a trunk?"

I peered at him. He was about two inches taller than I, an older man with smiley wrinkles, brown-framed glasses, and thick, white hair. He looked nice, except that his left eye twitched. I felt uneasy. "Well, yes, but...."

"I'm very interested in trunks. In fact, I have quite a few, and I restore them." He straightened his blue plaid tie and pulled on the lapels of his beige sports jacket.

"Restore them?"

"Yes—fix them up, you know. I replace the broken parts, repaint them. You said you found a trunk?"

Alia's sister Alistair broke into the group. "Alia, it's time to go. Dad's waiting in the car. It's apple pie day."

Alia tugged on my jeans' belt loop. "Umm, sorry, sir. We've got to go. Thanks for...."

We hurried up the aisle and out the church door. Alia's dad was waiting in front with the motor running. We got into the car and sat down. Alia looked at me, and I looked at her. We didn't have to say anything. We knew what the other was thinking: Someone else was interested in our trunk!

6

CORE OF
THE PROBLEM

The Millers invited me to lunch. I just went on home with them, figuring I'd call Mom from their house. She said that was fine and that I'd lucked out since Dad was making a typical Dad lunch—Spaghettios, pickles, and chips. Dad was good with barbecue but not too creative with the can opener.

"But, Annie," she said, "hurry home. You have to stack the wood today. You've been putting that off for a couple weeks now."

Ugh. Mom was just a bundle of fun.

Just as I got off the phone, the doorbell rang. I opened it since I was the closest. It was Maria. She wore stretchy black shorts and a plain white T-shirt, and her hair was flopped up on her head in a fabric tie.

"I couldn't stand it, wondering if you guys were checking out the keys, so I rode my blades over." I looked down. She was wearing Rollerblades. "Oops, I guess I'd better take these off. So, have you guys looked at the keys yet?"

Alia joined us from changing. She tucked her white T-shirt into cutoff jeans, and swooshed her hair up into a claw-like clip. "No, we just got home."

"Alia! Lunch!" Alia's mom peered out of the kitchen. "Hi, Maria. Want something to eat?"

Maria said she was famished, so we all went to the kitchen. Mrs. Miller had great-looking grilled cheeses ready, but what really caught my eye was Mr. Miller. He was already elbow deep in apple peels.

"Boy, someone must really want a lot of apples for lunch," I said.

Mrs. Miller laughed. "Oh, no, Annie. Rob is peeling apples for apple pies. Did you hear the announcement at church about the pie fest tonight?"

I nodded. "Yeah, what is that?"

"Well, we sell pies by the slice and by the pie as a fund-raiser for the youth. Rob and I make a half dozen or more every year together."

Mr. Miller laughed. "This year she bought me this Handy Dandy Apple Peeler and Corer"—he showed me the official name on the box—"so we're shooting for a dozen pies."

Mrs. Miller playfully pretended to put a long apple peel halo on Mr. Miller's head. "That's right. Isn't he an angel? I make the crusts. He peels the apples. Quite a team, huh?"

I sighed. They were a team. In fact, their whole household seemed like a lot of fun. Not like my house. I mean, Mom and Dad loved each other. But lately there'd been arguments and "Annie do this" and "Annie do that." There wasn't much fun anymore in the Shepard house. I sighed again. Too bad Mom and Dad weren't more like the Millers.

We girls scarfed our sandwiches and headed for Alia's room. There she pulled out two shoe boxes, each filled with smaller boxes. Each box had a certain type of key in it. Big old keys. Small old keys. Big new keys. Small new keys. Numbered keys. Unnumbered keys.

Alia was an organizer. You could tell that by her room. Everything had a place. That wasn't too weird. I mean, everything in my room had a place too. But my stuff was never in its place. Her stuff was. And everything was labeled. Shoe boxes were marked: blue boots, black flats, hiking boots. Her clothes hung neatly in a row in her closet—blouses, pants, dresses each in their allotted spot. Sweaters neatly folded on a shelf.

It made me sick. But the key collection was great. Each key was in a plastic Baggie marked with a label that said the date she got the key, the place, and if she knew, what it was for.

"Hands off," she said. "Each one goes in a certain place. That's why I didn't want to just hand this over. But let's take this to your place and see if something will work."

It seemed like she had every key that was ever made. Certainly one of them would open the trunk. As we started down the hall with the shoe boxes, Mrs. Miller popped her head out the kitchen.

"Where are you girls headed?"

"To Annie's, Mom. Alia found a trunk in a secret attic above her room. It's locked and we want to see if one of my keys will open it."

"A trunk? Mmmmmm. Sounds interesting." Alia's mom scratched her head. "Mountain Center Antiques has been running a want ad in the paper for trunks. I think it said they'd pay from fifty to a hundred dollars or more for a trunk."

Alia's dad came out of the kitchen munching on an apple core. "And doesn't John at church look for trunks too?"

"That's right," Alia's mom said. "He restores them beautifully. He donated one once for our Christmas bazaar raffle."

Alia and I looked at each other with a knowing nod.

"Rob, isn't there a local legend about a trunk?" Alia's mom snitched some of her husband's cored apple pieces.

"That's right! Some people say some gold miner hit a big vein of gold, mined it all out, but left a fortune in a trunk when his fiancée left him. He disappeared from town one day on his horse, never to be heard from again. And people have been looking for the trunk ever since."

I looked at Maria. Maria looked at me, then we both looked at Alia.

I gulped. "So trunks are pretty popular around here?"

"Yeah," said Mr. Miller. "I think that any trunk could be the one that holds the lost Mountain Center fortune. Maybe you have something there, Annie."

"Well, this certainly sounds like a fun little project," giggled Mrs. Miller.

"Mom, this is not a project. It's a case. We're sleuths. And this could be important. So, is it okay if I go over to Annie's?"

"Of course. But be back before dark. You are definitely not licensed to practice sleuthing after dark." Mrs. Miller tried to hold back a smile.

I knew she was poking fun at us, but it was okay. We had the trunk. And we maybe had the key. And maybe the lost Mountain Center fortune was in my room waiting for me to claim it as my own.

7

STACK ATTACK

"Maybe that's why it was so heavy," said Maria. She was pulling on my right arm.

"Yeah," said Alia. "Maybe we really do have the lost Mountain Center fortune in that trunk." She was pulling on my left arm.

"Whoa, you guys! Take it easy."

Both of them were rollerblading on either side of me. I was riding Alia's little sister's skateboard, and they were pulling me along. In their free hand each carried one of the two shoe boxes with the keys. It was working…sort of. The problem was Alia's skinny little legs could not pump along as fast as Maria's, and I felt as though I were on the rack, being stretched, only in jerks.

Ugh. "Whoa, Maria!" Ugh. "Come on, Alia." Ugh. We stopped at the end of my gravel road and walked the short distance to my house. Mom was getting in the car as we arrived. "I'm just going to check the animals at the store. Your dad and Link are scouting out hay. Annie, you've put off stacking that wood long enough. I need it done today."

Today? "But, Mom, we've got to...."

"Absolutely not, Annie. Before you get started on something else, get it done. Now!" She smiled, acknowledging Maria and Alia. "Hi, girls. Maybe you could give Annie a hand." And then she was off.

Mothers! They could be so embarrassing. I'd finally made a couple of friends, and then Mom barks at me in front of them. Total humiliation.

Maria and Alia looked at me in understanding for an awkward moment.

Maria broke the silence. "So, where's this wood?"

Alia smiled. "Yeah, let's do it!"

I led them around the side of the house to the big stack. After a couple of splinters, I found some work gloves, and we then began to work more efficiently. It was kind of tricky, since Maria and Alia still had on their Rollerblades. But we formed an assembly line, with Alia at the end, perfectly lining up the wood against the side of the house, so it couldn't topple. We even raked up the remaining wood chips.

"Boy, we made quick work of this," said Alia, scooping up the last of the chips. "Your mom...."

"Hey, Annie," said Maria, "who's this driving up?"

I looked around the side of the house. "I don't know anyone who has a small blue pickup." And then I recognized him. It was....

Alia gasped. "The man from church who asked about the trunk. What'll we do? What'll we say?"

"I bet he knows about the lost Mountain Center fortune," said Maria. "And I bet he's after it."

He got out of the car and walked up the front porch steps—obviously not noticing us at the side of the house—and knocked on the door.

I frowned. "A nice old man from church? Maybe he just wants to help. Maybe he's just curious. Maybe he just likes trunks. Maybe he won't even notice us if we're quiet, and he will just go away."

Alia's eyes widened. "Maybe he knows we're alone, and maybe he's going to hack us up and put us in the trunk and, and...."

"Quit, Alia." Maria made a cutoff sign across her throat. "You read too many newspaper articles. He's probably a nice old man like Annie said.... Oh, hi, there, sir."

The man had apparently heard our babbling and peered around the side of the porch. He wore tan slacks and a navy zip-up jacket. "No one else home?" He took off his tan canvas fishing hat and scratched his head.

We shook our heads. I cleared my voice. "Umm, gee, no, sir. But we, ah, expect anyone, someone home real, uh, soon. They just come and go—zip, zip—just like that. Any moment now someone could be coming right up that road and be here. My father, my mother—or my very tall older brother. Any of them." I smiled weakly.

He sighed. "Too bad. I was just interested in that trunk you mentioned at church today. You see, I do a lot of research about trunks. And restoration. It's quite a passion of mine." He looked over his shoulder, as though he'd heard someone coming.

At the word *passion* I felt an even bigger knot in my stomach. Maybe he was a nut case. And then another thought came to mind. "How did you know where I live?" I looked around. Alia had leaned the rake back against the back wall. I picked up a log and rested it on the pile, picking at the bark. It would make an awkward, but still formidable weapon.

"Excuse me?" he asked, looking back at me, his left eye twitching.

"How did you know where I live?"

Maria and Alia took my cue and each picked up a log, resting theirs on the pile and picking at the bark.

"Oh, that. I just asked around, and someone said you were the Shepards' girl. And everyone knows your family. And this house. But if your folks aren't home, I'll come another time. Goodbye, young ladies."

"And your name?" I called after him. But I guess he was hard of hearing as he didn't answer or even turn around.

I laid the log back on the pile. "One thing is for sure." I looked at Maria and Alia. "Trunks are a popular thing around here."

Alia picked up her two shoe boxes and smiled. "So what are we waiting for?"

My two friends took off their rollerblades, and we all ran up the porch steps, into the house and up the sixteen steps to my room. I took the lamp off the trunk and tugged it away from the wall and bed a little.

"Okay," said Alia. "Let's go about this systematically." She began removing little boxes from the shoe box and lining them up on the bed in a row. "Little keys. Big keys. Old keys...."

"Alia!" I yelled. "I can't believe this. Just gimme the keys and let's try them. A fortune could be in that trunk!"

"Now, now," said Maria, coming between us. "We know it's got to be an old key. So let's just start with the old keys. Alia, you dish 'em out. Hand one to me, and I'll hand it to Annie. She'll try it. While she's trying it, you can get the next one ready and hand it to me. Then Annie will hand the first one back to me, and I'll hand her the second one and the first one back to you. Then you can get the third ready..."

Ahhhhhhh! I couldn't take it any longer. "Quit!" I said. "Let's just get going before some other trunk hunter comes along and snatches this away from us."

I had to admit it. We were a pretty good team. Alia was a good organizer of things, Maria was a good organizer of people, and I was the idea man...or woman...or whatever. As Alia handed over the first key, I smiled. It worked like clockwork. My team handed the keys over one by one. I tried them, one by one. The lock did not budge. None of the old keys worked. We even tried the new keys, large keys, small keys, etcetera keys. None of them worked, either.

"I thought for sure one of these would work." I flopped back on the dozen blue pillows on my floor. "They are the most keys I've ever seen in one place. How could they all not work?" I sat up. "I'm getting mad at this trunk thing." I stood up. "In fact, I'm so mad at this trunk, I'm going to kick it." I kicked at the lock. "Maybe the stupid thing would just give and...."

"Annie, stop!" Maria stood up. "Stop! If this trunk does have the lost Mountain Center fortune in it, it's worth something just in itself. Or the least it's worth is fifty to hundred dollars or more, according to Alia's dad. Remember?"

I did remember. I sat down again. "But not without a key, Maria. We've got to get it open. If only we had another couple hundred keys."

"That's it!" said Alia.

"What?" I asked.

"I know where there are a couple hundred or more keys— at the museum."

"The museum?" I rubbed my toes.

"The museum downtown has an old key collection. We at least now know what type of key it's got to be—an old, short one with just a few notches at the end. Let's go scout it out tomorrow and see if maybe the museum will let us borrow some."

I smiled. "Alia, you are positively brilliant. Okay, that's the plan. We go to the museum tomorrow after school to check out the keys. We'll have to come up with some kind of story to talk the museum people out of the keys for a day. What should we tell them?"

Maria and Alia looked at me strangely. "Duh," they both said.

Oh, I got it. The truth. I mean, what stranger story could you come up with than a mysterious trunk found in the attic of an antique house that could possibly hold the lost Mountain Center fortune?

"I get it, guys. I guess the truth is stranger than fiction, huh?"

Maria looked at Alia and Alia looked back at her. At the very same moment they broke into country song again: "Fiction is no stranger than truth…I lost my tooth…when I married Ruth…"

Ahhhhhh! Not their singing again! I grabbed Alia's key collection and motioned as though I were going to toss it out the window. That put a stop to that singing nonsense.

We hadn't realized that the sun was slipping behind the mountain and the shadows were forming all over the place. We went downstairs to the porch where Maria and Alia put their Rollerblades back on. Soon they were off tiptoeing down the gravel road, Alia holding the shoe boxes and Maria holding the skateboard. They started off on their country song again, and I clapped my hands over my ears. They were a weird pair. But perhaps tomorrow the three of us would find the key to my trunk problem.

8

MUSEUM MUSINGS

After school Monday we hurried to the museum. I was surprised that I hadn't noticed the old building, obviously converted from an old two-story house with big bay windows and a wrap-around porch, right behind the county courthouse. We walked up the long walkway, bordered on either side by neatly trimmed, box-like bushes that formed walls for two small rose gardens.

As I pushed open the heavy oak door, a tiny bell rang. Almost instantly an elf-like person with a gray-haired bun stood in front of me. Her badge said: "Docent Dora."

"W-w-welcome to the Mountain Center Museum," she monotoned. "We have a variety of displays about local history. To your left you will notice..."

I looked at Maria and Alia, and we shrugged our shoulders simultaneously. This little wisp of a woman in a long, brown print, pioneer-type dress had a prerecorded speech that apparently she was going to continue unless we could somehow delicately stop her.

"Umm, excuse me, m'am," I whispered.

"...and we have a fine collection of Native American baskets in this display to your left which include...."

Why was everyone so hard of hearing? Did our mile-high Sierras elevation block people's eardrums? I stepped right in front of her wrinkled little face. "M'am, we just...."

"...several examples of Washoe Indian workmanship as well as our own...." She stopped. "Did you say something?"

Whew! "Yes, m'am, we're just interested in keys."

"Keys?" She switched gears and turned around, pointing to the stairs. "On the second floor you will find the Huntington Key Collection, donated by the family of...."

Maria and Alia must have had the same thought as I did, because we each started softly for the stairs while Docent Dora continued. After a few moments she noticed that we were heading up the stairs but still kept on with her prerecorded message. As we reached the top of the stairs, we peeked over the railing. Yep, Docent Dora was still droning her address.

But someone else caught my eye. In a corner of the first floor the man from church was working at a table. He had several books laid out in front of him and was taking notes on a yellow pad.

I ducked down below the banister and pulled on Maria's and Alia's shirts. We were patriotic that day—each of us in blue jeans and T-shirts. Maria's red, Alia's white, and mine blue.

Behind him the walls held collections of stone and other Indian tools, baskets, and a life-size diorama of Native people. On the other side of the room, stuffed animals and birds stood watch. Off the main room were two doors—one "Closed for Exhibit Work" and the other signed "1880 Kitchen."

"Look at this!" I pointed through the rails.

"Oh, no," said Alia. "That's him!"

"What is he doing here?" said Maria.

I put my finger to my mouth. "Maybe he's after the same thing we are."

"In books?" said Maria.

"Yeah, I don't think so," said Alia. "It's probably just a weird coincidence. Let's go find the keys."

Just behind us along the wall we found them. The large collection was under a locked glass display case.

"There are all kinds of them—a couple hundred, at least," said Alia. "Any one of these might work."

She was right. They were all old, many of them with just a few notches at the end.

"Now what?" said Maria. "Hit up Docent Dora for a donation?"

"She'd probably have the key to the keys," I said.

"Yes," said Alia, "I think the key to getting our key is to ask Docent Dora for the key to the keys so we can borrow the keys to find out if one of these keys...."

"Alia!" I tapped my foot, trying not to grin, and motioned them back down the stairs. But we had another problem now. We didn't want to let the man from church see us. Docent

Dora was dusting books at the gift counter now, which was a clear shot down the aisle from where the man from church was sitting. If he turned his head, he would see us at the counter.

I stood on the bottom step, where his view of me was blocked by a display of large hanging quilts.

"Pssst! Pssst!"

Deaf Docent Dora looked up and around. She looked back at her dusting.

"Ahem! Ahem!"

She looked up again, this time catching my eye and motioning hand and tiptoeing over to where we were on the stairs.

"May I help you?"

I backed up a couple of steps to make sure we couldn't be seen. "Miss Dora, we really need to borrow some of the keys in your Huntington Key Collection. You see, I found this trunk in my attic, but it's locked. And we don't have the key, and I just know there's something in it and...."

Docent Dora looked as though she'd seen a ghost. "Did you say you found a trunk?"

"Oh, no, here we go again," whispered Alia.

"Are you aware that the lost Mountain Center fortune could be in that trunk? Local legend has it that a gold miner abandoned all his gold when he was spurned by the woman he loved, and that when he died, she locked up all her memories of him, including the remainder of his fortune, now said to be worth over a million dollars."

She turned around and peered across the room. "In fact,

that gentleman over there is doing research at this very moment about that tale. I bet he would be very interested in your story about a trunk. I'll just go ask him to come speak to you...."

"Oh, no, m'am," I said. "We just want to borrow your keys. We'll be very careful with them. We'll count them before we go and put them all right back where they go."

"Oh, my goodness, no," said Dora. "We don't ever loan out any of our collections, except of course to school teachers and librarians in special cases. And you're certainly not a teacher now, are you?" She stood there with her hands folded together.

We shook our heads. Nothing was going our way. It seemed like the only way we were going to open the trunk was with a chisel. And then I had another thought. There was someone who might be able to borrow the collection. And if we hurried, we could get there and get back to the museum before it closed.

9

R&R

"I know just what we need," I said as we walked down the museum's walk back to the street.

"What?" Maria and Alia said.

"Some R and R."

They looked at me, puzzled.

"Some rest and relaxation." I smiled. "Grandma Rose."

They smiled back. They knew Grandma Rose's house would be a retreat away from our problems with the keys and trunk and weird people trying to get it away from us. Her home was like a Victorian cottage, with rose prints on the walls and draperies and light scents wafting from room to room.

We hurried the few blocks from the museum down a side street past the church to her home. The rose-covered vines were finally beginning to wilt with the colder, late September nights. It made her house look as though it were wrinkled, older, sadder. But I knew things would be just as happy as always inside. Grandma Rose never changed—she was always happy, warm, welcoming.

I knocked on the door. No answer. I knew she was home. I could hear the teapot whistling in the kitchen. That was weird. Grandma Rose always took her tea water off immediately because she said the water was best when it first boiled.

I rang the bell. I heard a meow and the hustling of feet. Suddenly Grandma Rose whisked open the door. At least I thought it was Grandma Rose. In front of me stood a woman in a long pink bathrobe and curlers.

"Annie! Sorry, dear, I didn't hear you at first."

"Grandma Rose?" I couldn't believe it. I'd never seen Grandma Rose in anything but real clothes—and her hair was always put together just so, usually under a floppy hat with roses on it. But there she stood looking as though she'd just gotten up.

"Excuse me, dear, I'm getting ready for an occasion." She opened the door, nonetheless, inviting us in with a sweep of her hand that was holding a pair of pantyhose.

"Oops!" She noticed the pantyhose. "Just let me get rid of these, and I'll be right with you. Go on in the kitchen and pour yourselves some tea. The water's ready."

I took the whistling pot off the burner and found some teacups and loose tea. Maria and Alia sat at her kitchen table. *Now where is the thingamabob you put the tea in?* I looked through her cupboards and sighed. Usually when I visited Grandma Rose, she would give me the red carpet treatment, often making her special fruit whirlies.

God, what is happening with my family? Even Grandma Rose!

I didn't even get a hug.

I found the tea thingamabob and poured the spiced tea into it and set it into the teapot. Grandma Rose appeared. "So what are you ladies up to?"

Up to? Maria and Alia scrunched up their faces. That made it sound like we were troublemakers. Grandma Rose was not quite herself. Even so, as I set the teacups on the table and poured the tea, I explained about the attic and the trunk.

Alia stirred her tea. "And boy was her mom mad when Annie broke her Great-Aunt Maudie's table."

Uh-oh. That was the wrong thing to say.

"My sister Maudie?"

Alia gulped. And I tried to explain about the accidental demise of the antique table. Grandma Rose seemed to understand, but this was not setting things up well for my request.

I told her about how we needed a key and how none of Alia's keys worked. "So we went to the museum to look at the key collection there, but we couldn't check it out. But the lady there said TEACHERS could check it out." I paused, letting the weight of my words fall into place.

Maria sipped her tea. "Grandma Rose, you were a TEACHER once, weren't you?"

"Yes, dear, I was. An English teacher. Teaching is an honorable profession. A high calling." She looked into space for a moment in thought.

I knew what was coming.

"But where's the man, who counsel can bestow,
   Still pleas'd to teach, and yet not proud to know?"

"Shakespeare?" I guessed.

"No," Grandma Rose said, sipping her tea. Alexander Pope. *An Essay on Criticism*." She sipped the tea again. "Oops, heavens, no, *An Essay on Man*. Silly me."

"That's okay, Grandma Rose," said Alia. "You're forgiven."

"To err is human, to forgive, divine," Grandma Rose said.

"Shakespeare?" I guessed again.

"No, Pope once again," she said. "Same essay."

"Good stuff," said Maria, sipping her tea.

"Yes, I like Pope," said Grandma Rose.

Maria, Alia and I exchanged glances. We all knew Maria meant the tea, not the writer.

I had to come out with it. "So, Grandma Rose, since you were a teacher, do you think you could call the museum and see if they'd let you check out the key collection. You know, so we could try the keys on the trunk?"

Grandma Rose looked at me with her eyes dancing playfully. She'd been teasing me, making me ask the question outright. "Of course, dear. Let's do it tomorrow. I would today, but I'm in the middle of this special occasion."

"So, Grandma Rose," I said, "what is this thing you're getting all spiffed up for? A Bible study? A ladies' circle meeting?"

"Well, Annie, this may come as a surprise, but I have a date."

A date? My mouth dropped to Australia.

"A date?"

Maria and Alia looked as surprised as I. "A date?" they echoed.

"With a man?" I asked.

"With a man. You may have met him at church yesterday. His name is John Cornwall. He's a very nice man. In fact, you and he have a common interest." She poured some more tea into her cup. "Hmmmm. What a funny coincidence you came by today with that story of yours. He's quite interested in trunks. He collects them, repairs them. Who knows, he might even have trunk keys. Now that I think about it, you should just stick around here, so you can meet him."

I swallowed hard and choked, and all of a sudden tea came spurting out of my nose.

"Ooo, gross," said Alia, covering her mouth.

"Oh, my goodness." Grandma Rose handed me a cloth napkin and mopped up the table with another. "Did I say something odd?"

I sneezed out some more tea. "Umm, uh, no, Grandma Rose. It's just that we're already running late and so we have to run, because we're running late, you see. So we have to go."

In about two more sneezes we were out the door.

"That was pretty lame," said Maria, as we headed down the walk. "We could have found out something about this John…what was his name?"

"Cornwall," I said. "John Cornwall. You're right. I guess I BLEW my cover."

"Or achooed it," said Alia. "At least we know his name now."

I sneezed again. "Another doo-doo doo-doo thing. Or do you think he could be dating Grandma Rose to find out something about my trunk?"

All of a sudden I got a sick feeling in my stomach. If the lost Mountain Center fortune were really in my trunk and if it were really worth a million dollars, someone like John Cornwall might do anything to get it. *Con men, bad people take advantage of old folks all the time—steal their money, rob their savings with phony schemes. Grandma Rose might be in danger. Somehow, we have to do something to stop that date from ever taking place.*

At that moment rest and relaxation had just turned to wretch and revulsion.

10

REEL OR NOT

"Annie, you just can't go interfering in your grandmother's love life," said Maria.

We were walking home when I looked up and noticed we were approaching Reel Real Estate.

"But it's kind of odd how Mr. Cornwall would take an interest in her just as we have this trunk case," said Alia.

I sighed. "I just feel I should warn her somehow."

"Coincidences can just happen," said Maria. "You just bump into someone at the right..."

Screeeeech! Thunk! Ugh!

Suddenly I was sitting flat on the sidewalk next to a large hedge, lights buzzing around the edges of my eyes. I shook my head. I was looking straight at the neon orange—Esther Reel. She and her bicycle had thunked into me as they emerged from a driveway next to the hedge.

"Oh, my goodness gracious, I've just clobbered one of my angels of mercy! I'm so sorry. I'm so sorry." Esther tried to get up, but it's hard to get up when a bicycle is on top of you. Maria and Alia stood the bike up, and Esther clambered to her feet, reaching down to give me a hand.

"Hello, Mrs. Reel." I brushed off my jeans and picked up my backpack. "It's all right—my backpack cushioned me."

"Well, it was pretty silly of me to come thundering out of my office driveway without looking. And you girls were so nice to me the other night. There must be some way I can do something nice for you." She paused for a moment and brushed herself off.

I thought. There was.

"Mrs. Reel, if we found something in my house that was left there, you know, by the former owners, whose would it be? The former owners or ours, since we found it?" I forced a smile to be polite.

"Have you found something?"

"Well, I'm not sure. Yes, I guess. It's a personal item. It doesn't have any apparent value."

"What is it?"

"It's just an unimportant thing, really. But that shouldn't matter, should it? Is it mine or the former owner's?"

The neon orange eyed me carefully from behind her owl-like glasses. "It's a trunk, isn't it? A trunk was rumored to be in the house. I looked all over but never found it."

I squirmed a little and fidgeted with my backpack straps. "I didn't say what it was."

"I would have to look at the contract of sale in my file. The former owner? I can't even remember the name, actually. The house had been vacant a long time before it was sold. Everything was handled through a trustee—some highfalutin businessman. Never actually met the man. We did everything through the mail. I'll have to check my records. I'll need to see the item or items also. I'll be calling you." She got back on her bicycle. "Hmm, a trunk...well, isn't that interesting. Wait'll I tell..."

And she was off. We started down the street too.

"Annie," said Maria, "you're giving everything away. Every person in this whole town is going to know about that trunk. You're going to have every fortune seeker this side of the Sierra knocking on your door."

"Yes," said Alia, "this trunk is becoming some hot tamale around town."

"Hot tamale?" Maria smiled. "That reminds me—the whole family is making tamales at home for the Mexican dinner at church."

I looked at her quizzingly. "Maria, you go to church? I didn't know that."

"Well, yeah—the whole family does. It's just a Martinez thing. And we always make tamales for the Mexican dinner. It's next weekend. But, c'mon to my house—you gotta see this."

Maria's house was just a couple blocks away. And she was right—it was a sight to see. Maria's mom had a whole crew, assembly-line style, along her kitchen counter.

"*Hola, mamá,*" Maria said as we went in the back door. Then she turned to us, "This is Aunt Josefina, Aunt Celia, and Grandma Teresa. You know my mom and dad."

After a lot of holas, we got the rookie's course on tamale

making. Josefina picked a moist cornhusk from a pile and spread the masa dough on it in a rectangle. She then passed it to Celia who spooned the meat filling on top of the dough. She then passed it to Maria's mom who rolled it up like a jelly roll, tied the ends and set it on a rack in a large steamer.

Maria said they'd been at it most of the day and would prepare hundreds for the church dinner. With a few hungry moans and sucked-in, hungry-looking cheeks, we begged one each and messily munched them with our fingers as we sat on the kitchen floor.

"*Apurrate, Juanita*," said Celia to Maria's mom, "*estamos atrasadas por tu culpa.*"

"*Si,*" said Josefina, "*nunca vamos a terminar esto.*"

I shrugged my shoulders at Maria.

"They're telling my mom to hurry up," whispered Maria. "They always tease each other like that. If they didn't, I'd think something was wrong." She smiled.

The tamale was yummy—spicy hot too. The whole Martinez home was warm, in fact—a busy, fun kind of place. I thought of my own family. It seemed like we never did anything together anymore. Link was a junior at high school and was either studying, working at the feed store, or dating or talking with Crystal, his girlfriend. Mom and Dad were either at the feed store or at the dining room table working on the business books. We hardly ever all ate dinner together or did anything together but work at the feed store. And even there, we each had separate tasks.

Home just didn't seem like home anymore. It was just a big house with a lot of separate rooms. We didn't have friends yet here in Mountain Center that we'd have to dinner or just over for cards like in L.A. No, it was just a big, lonely place—a house, not a home. And our family didn't seem like a family anymore.

"Annie..."

I sighed as I watched Maria's aunts and grandmother teasing each other at the counter. I'd never had a family like that. And probably never would. *God, why can't I have a family like Maria's or Alia's? One that, you know, is more together?*

"Annie!" Alia was practically in my face. "Alia to Annie. You in there?"

I nodded. "Just thinking, okay?" I munched another bite. "Yumm, this is good."

Alia licked her fingers. "Sure is. I was just telling Maria about youth night at our church. Do you guys want to go? It's Wednesday night."

"Sure," I said, licking my fingers, too. "Maria?"

"I'll let you know later. But I did get an idea just now. Why don't we call a locksmith about the key to the trunk? Maybe he'd have just the thing...you know, in case it doesn't work out with your grandma, Annie."

"Cool idea," I said. "Let's see—it's probably too late to call now. Let's do it tomorrow at school, then we could still go with Grandma Rose after school. Okay?"

Maria and Alia grinned back. They were funny looking with the cruddies stuck in their teeth from the tamales. And then I thought of Grandma Rose. *She could be on her way right now with that John Cornwall. God? Could you please keep an eye on my grandma? If he's only interested in the hot tamale trunk, she could get hurt. Okay, God?*

11

A LEAD
ON THE LOCK

We parted ways at Maria's house. I tossed and turned all night long, wondering and worrying about Grandma Rose. When I woke up Tuesday morning, I called her, but I got no answer. I thought it unusual that she would be gone so early in the morning. I wanted to go check on her myself, but I didn't have time before school.

I moseyed down to the kitchen where Mom was emptying the dishwasher. "Mom, have you heard from Grandma Rose lately?"

"Not since, let's see, about Saturday." She turned to look at me. "Why?"

"Oh, I don't know. When I stopped by her house yesterday, she was all set to go out somewhere...." I instantly decided not to tell her about Gram's "occasion." "And she's not home this morning—I just called."

"That's not unusual. She could be walking or having a cup of tea with someone." Mom continued cleaning up.

"At 7:30?"

She paused again, staring for a second. "You're right. It is a little early for her to be out. I'll give her a call from the store this morning." She smiled at me. "It's nice for you to show concern about your grandmother. Are you worried about something, Annie?"

"Oh, no," I said, pouring a bowl of cereal. "She was just on my mind."

I still didn't feel too good about a lot of things a dozen minutes later as I met up with Maria and Alia on the way to school.

"Annie, look at this!" Maria was waving the local newspaper, *The Mountain Center Messenger*.

"What?"

"There are a couple ads in the paper I thought you'd be interested in. First, read this."

I took the paper from her. I read the ad she pointed out. "Local City Locksmith. We've got the key to your problem. Call 231-0204."

"Cool," said Alia. "Another coincidence, huh? Life is sure full of 'em."

"Yeah," said Maria. "And look at this ad." She pointed just below the locksmith ad.

"Mountain Center Antiques," I read. "You'll treasure our treasures. Two forty-one Main Street. Mountain Center. Hours: 10 A.M. to 5 P.M., Tuesday through Saturday."

"So?" asked Alia.

"That's not it," said Maria. "Here, read the print along the edge of the ad.

I turned the paper sideways and read the small print along the border. "Turn your trash in for cash." I turned the paper as I read. "Especially looking for Depression glassware...furniture of all kinds...and trunks. We pay top dollar."

"See?" said Maria. "Trunks!"

"Do you think that's the guy who came by the house the other night. The jogger?" I handed the paper back to Maria.

"I'm sure of it," said Maria.

"Another coincidence," said Alia, nodding her head.

Honk! I turned to look. It was Link in his new, old pickup truck pulling over behind us. He caught the good looks of the Italian side of the family—the Martonis, Mom's side. Tall, dark, and handsome described Link. Maria and Alia said every girl at Mountain Center High drooled when he walked in the first day of school.

"Hey, Squirt, you forgot your backpack." He leaned out the passenger side window and dropped it into my arms. "And Mom says don't forget to clean cages this afternoon. She has that doctor appointment."

"Thanks." I stuck my tongue out. How could Link so effectively embarrass me every time in front of my friends?

"Why does he call you Squirt?" asked Alia. "I mean, you are five feet eight, aren't you? You're about a whole head taller than I am."

"I don't know. I think it's a boy thing. Like he's reminding me he's the big brother." I sighed. "Lately it seems everyone in my family is on my case." I thought for a moment. "Do they let kids divorce their families?"

"I read about that once in the paper," said Maria. "Some girl really did. Kind of sad."

We walked the rest of the way to school in a mopey silence. Sometimes friends know just what to say. And sometimes friends know not to say anything at all. At least I had two friends who were cool enough not to say anything when that was just what I needed at the time.

At lunchtime we met at the school pay phone.

"Got the number?" I asked Maria.

"Right here." She handed me the newspaper. I dialed the number. Then I hung up.

"What?" said Maria.

"I need to rehearse what I'm going to say," I said. "I always do that. Then I don't sound like an idiot."

"So rehearse," said Maria.

"Hmm...okay....hmmm...tum...tum...tum...." I breathed in deeply. "Okay, I'm ready."

Maria and Alia looked at each other in total amazement. I guess they'd never seen anyone rehearse before.

I dialed the number again. A man answered. "Local City Locksmith."

I explained my problem and paused, taking mental notes of his instructions, then hung up.

"What did he say?" said Maria.

"He said to check the lock and see if it has the name of a lock company on it and a number. If it does, he may be able to give me a key that will work without even looking at it. Otherwise, he'll have to take the trunk to his shop. I'm supposed to call him back."

"Well, that sounds good," said Alia.

"Well, yeah," I said, "if there's a number. Then it will just cost for the key. If he has to make a house call, it'll cost fifty dollars plus time on the job to make a key."

"Y'ouch," said Maria. "I hope whatever is in that trunk is worth all this effort."

We all agreed to go to my house after school. As I thought about it, I got a flippy feeling in my stomach again. It was possible that in just a couple of hours we would be able to unlock the trunk and find out if we really did have the lost Mountain Center fortune.

12

A SNOOP

"Hurry up, Alia." I paused for a second as we turned onto Fairgrounds Road.

"Yeah, hurry up," said Maria, who had paced us home from school.

"I'm coming, I'm coming," huffed Alia. "I'm going as fast as my little tennies will take me. Just 'cause you two are bigger doesn't mean you should...."

"Ssshhhh!" I pointed ahead and tried to hide behind a tree at the front corner of my yard. A somewhat familiar bicycle was leaning against the front porch. And going around the left side of the house was Esther Reel.

Maria and Alia hid behind me as I peered around the tree. The realtor had gone from view. I put my finger to my lips and motioned my friends to follow me. We all quietly set our backpacks down on the ground. Alia got a worried look on her face, but Maria pulled her along by her sleeve.

But Alia planted her feet firmly. "We need a signal."

"A what?" I whispered.

"A signal," said Alia. "In case we get cornered. How about this? One-two-three," she raised her fingers one at a time, "then we scream."

"Okay," I said. "Whatever, Alia. One-two-three: That's our signal."

She sighed with a faint smile.

We crept to the edge of the front porch. Esther Reel was on her tiptoes, trying to peek into a side window. But she was a bit too short so she grabbed a log from the woodpile at the back end of the house and used it like a stepstool. She put her hands on either side of her eyes to shade out the sun's glare. Then she shook her head a little and moved to the next window and did the same thing.

"She's looking for the trunk," said Maria. "I bet she knows what's in it."

"Sh-sh-she probably thought everyone would be either at work or at school," said Alia.

I nodded in agreement. Maybe she had talked with the former owner or—what was that word?—trustee? Maybe she did find out what secret the trunk hid.

"You two head her off around front," I said. "Don't let her see you until I give you the signal."

Maria and Alia went back around front. I heard their soft footsteps on the front porch, and a board squeaked. Great. But Esther, deep in thought, obviously hadn't heard, as she walked up the steps to our back porch. She tried the back door handle and frowned. It was locked. Mom and Dad still had their L.A. habits in place and kept the doors locked, even though many Mountain Center people didn't.

Esther stopped for a moment as she descended the stairs, looking first right, then left, as though she'd heard something. She put her right hand to her mouth and bit her nails. I was right. She was after something.

The neon orange looked around the other side of the house to see if the coast were clear. She apparently thought it was and tiptoed around, peering through those windows too.

Squeeeaaak. Oh, no. That was the front porch swing. Couldn't Maria and Alia take our sleuthing seriously and quietly follow orders?

Esther had heard it too and abruptly turned around. I quickly started to backtrack, looking for somewhere to hide. I could head for the brick barbeque at the patio or a tree in the yard. But it was too late to hide.

She had looked up and noticed me. And she jumped. "Oh, my goodness gracious, there you are. I was just l-l-looking for you."

"Around the back of the house?" I couldn't decide if she had jumped from surprise or nervous guilt.

"Oh, I thought maybe you'd be out back playing...."

"Playing?" It was a dumb question. I knew it. And I could tell she knew it.

"Oh, goodness gracious, of course you don't play. You're how old, umm, Amy?"

"My name's Annie." I knew she was changing the subject.

"Why were you looking for me?"

Maria and Alia leaned over the rail of the front porch. Their eyes bugged out.

"I, uh, just stopped by to tell you I wasn't, uh, able to reach the trustee for the former owner. He was not in his office in San Francisco—his secretary said he was on vacation. It seems to me that he vacationed somewhere near here—that's how we originally met, I think. So, I'm sorry I can't be of more help."

She started down the driveway and noticed that Maria and Alia had also been listening. She smiled weakly at them, then me, and stumbled over a small rock in the driveway. Then she got on her bicycle.

I tried to think of something to say to keep her from escaping, but my tongue tripped over in garbles. And then I heard the phone ringing inside the house.

"Shucks," I muttered, running up the porch steps and fumbling for my key in my jeans pocket. It was on a keychain that looked like a California license plate. I turned the key in the front door lock and pushed my weight against the door. After its normal instant of sticking, it gave way, and I ran inside for the phone on a table in the front hall.

As soon as I heard the voice, I remembered. "Annie!"

"Mom....oops....I know...cages....I'm sorry...I forgot....I'll be there in just....I said I'm sorry....I just..." The phone clicked. "...forgot."

I looked at Maria and Alia, standing just inside the front doorway. They had that "we know" look in their eyes.

And then the front steps squeaked again. "Hello! Anne, dear?

Open the screen door, would you?" It was Grandma Rose. "Guess what I've got?"

She was struggling with a wide, shallow cardboard box. Grandma Rose had probably been cleaning out her closets again. Boy, was this bad timing, or what? Mom was going to get even madder if I were any more late. I walked over and reached out to relieve her of the load. But as I casually looked into the box, I gulped.

Grandma Rose had what looked like the whole collection of keys from the Mountain Center Museum.

13

COINCIDENCES OR CIRCUMSTANCES

"I got them, Anne dear!" Grandma Rose was beaming from one hearing aid to another.

"Wow, Grandma Rose," I said, sitting on the inside stairway and resting the box on my knee, "how did you do it?"

"Well, I've got connections." She smiled, blushing just on the very centers of her cheeks.

"Connections?" asked Maria.

"You know Docent Dora?" said Alia.

"No, I mean, yes, I know Dora. But, more importantly, I know the museum curator."

"They make hams at the museum?" asked Alia.

Maria and I looked at each other. We just had to work on Alia's vocabulary before she got to high school.

"No, dear," explained Grandma Rose. "The curator at a museum is the person in charge of the whole collection. It just so happens that my new friend is John Cornwall, the museum director—the curator."

"The man from church?" I asked. "He's the museum curator?"

"The man who asked about Annie's trunk?" Alia was with it now.

"The same gentleman," said Grandma Rose. That explained why we had seen him at the museum the day before. "We had a lovely dinner out together last night, and I explained your new problem—excuse me, your case. He was quite willing to let me borrow the keys for the afternoon. In fact, he helped me gather them together early this morning. And, we're going to have dinner again tonight—at his house."

I picked up a key from the box. "I called you this morning, Grandma Rose. I guess that's where you were. I was a little...umm, fearful."

She gave me a funny little how-so look, then smiled it off. "Fearful, Annie? 'The fear of the Lord is the key to this treasure,'" she said. "Ha! That's appropriate, isn't it, Anne dear?"

"Another quote?" asked Maria.

"Yes—the Bible," said Grandma Rose. "Isaiah 33:6. Actually the whole verse says, 'He will be the sure foundation for your times, a rich store of salvation and wisdom and knowledge; the fear of the Lord is the key to this treasure.'"

"Grandma Rose! I'd really like to try these keys right now, but I've got to get to the feed store. I'm supposed to clean cages for Mom. She just called. She's gonna skin me if I'm not there in two shakes."

"Oh, dear, I wish I could give you a ride, but I promised John—Mr. Cornwall—that I'd not let these keys out of my sight. Why don't you hurry along and get the cleaning done, and Maria, Alia, and I will try these keys on your trunk. I gave him my word that I'd have them back before the museum closed today."

Reluctantly I hurried away on my bike to the feed store. It just seemed that every time I was hot onto some lead, Mom was right there, trying to mess things up. *You'd think I was her slave to be doing all the dirty jobs around the house and the store.* I thought again of Alia's family going to church and breakfast together and how her mom and dad made apple pies together. And then I thought of Maria's family and how their extended family made life in that household seem so comfortable and warm.

God, why have you stuck me with the family I have? I prayed as I glided up to the feed store. *Grandma Rose is cool, but no one else seems to understand or care. And if Grandma Rose is making a new "friend," that might mean she will have less time or concern for me.*

Link and Dad were rearranging hay, and Mom was busy with customers as I went in the back door. I started right in on the cages, emptying the dirtied shavings into the dumpster and putting fresh ones in the trays. The rabbits and hamsters and mice and others were used to me and shied away only momentarily as I approached each cage.

I was trying so hard to get things done quickly that I hardly noticed who had come into the shop. And then I heard his voice. It was the man from church—John Cornwall—

Grandma Rose's new friend. Another doo-doo doo-doo thing. I was beginning to think there weren't coincidences, but that God was orchestrating it all. I spied through a pass-through between the store and pet areas.

"Thank you, Mrs. Shepard," he was saying. "I hope this works—this rat poison. I'm certainly tired of all the pests around the museum. You're sure this will rid us of our problems?"

"Positive," Mom said. "We had a similar problem at our house when we moved in. It had been vacant for quite awhile, you know, so rodents had made it their home. But that Cure-All stuff definitely worked in a hurry."

"Fine. I'll take your word for it." John Cornwall started for the front door, then turned, pausing. "By the way, I met your daughter in church the other day. Lovely girl. She seems quite taken with a trunk you apparently found in your home."

"Oh, that." Mom picked up a duster and started brushing the stock on the shelves. "It's an old thing, that's certain. Probably has a lot of old junk in it."

"You still don't know? I mean, is it locked?"

Mom seemed surprised by his interest. "Why, yes, there doesn't seem to be a key to it. Why are...."

His eye twitched for a second, and he shook his head as if to clear his thoughts. And then without another word, John Cornwall left the store.

Mom watched him close the door. "Hmmm." She started after him a moment, then resumed her dusting.

I went back to my cages, finishing quickly and filing away every word I heard. Rat poison? *Pests?* Could that mean us?

Or Grandma Rose? Or all of us? He definitely still seemed curious about the trunk. People in small towns often struck up conversations easily but why mention a trunk out of the blue? Was he fishing again?

I just had to get home to tell Grandma Rose, no *warn* Grandma Rose about John Cornwall. His twitchy eye gave me the willies. And I didn't want her eating dinner at his house tonight. The dinner menu might be Pest Poison Potluck. Because if he were obsessed about the trunk, he might do away with anyone who had an interest in it. And that could mean Grandma Rose. Or Maria, Alia, and me.

14

SUSPICIONS

I was home in a hurry. Maria, Alia, and Grandma Rose were trying the last of the keys.

"Nope," said Alia, "too big." She gave the key to Maria who gave it to Grandma Rose. They had the old assembly line working again.

I instantly started tapping my foot. Alia had to keep each key in exactly the same spot in the box. *Picky, picky! Just do it, Alia!*

Maria rolled her eyes. I could tell she felt the same way.

Alia tried another. "Nope, too little."

A dozen or so keys later, Grandma Rose announced, "Well, that's it, girls. None of these worked. I guess that lock takes a special key."

Then I remembered the locksmith's instructions. "Let's see, is there a lock company name on the trunk?"

In small engraving at the bottom of the lock, there it was: "Hey, great! American Lock Co." And then I sighed. "But no lock number."

"Well, that limits things a little, at least," said Maria.

Grandma Rose got up slowly from her perch on one of my pillows on the floor. "Oooo, my poor old bones. Well, girls, I've got to get these keys back. Annie, could you help me to my car with them?"

I gathered the last of the keys and set them in place in the box. It was generous of John Cornwall to loan them to us. If he had bad intentions, why would he do that? If he wanted the trunk, surely he could just come get it and break it open. But somehow I just couldn't trust his looks.

As we approached Grandma Rose's brown and white '57 Chevy, she slowed. "Anne, dear, something seems to be on your mind. Didn't everything go well at the store? Are you having problems with your mother and dad?"

I turned to face her. She was good at reading faces and feelings. "It was nothing, really, Grandma Rose. Just an ordinary afternoon.... Except that your friend came in."

"Oh, which one?" She unlocked the front passenger door.

I opened it and set the box on the seat. "Your new friend— John Cornwall. He was buying rat poison."

Grandma Rose laughed. "Oh, of course. He mentioned the problem with the rodents at the museum."

I looked at her. She was flushed again. Could Grandma Rose be falling for this man? "Grandma Rose, are you sure he's okay? I mean, don't you think it's strange that he's interested in you just at the same time we find this trunk? He seemed so obsessed about our trunk the other day—and he mentioned it again at the feed store. I think...I think he believes there's a fortune in it and is using you to get to the trunk."

A sudden paleness washed over Grandma Rose's face. It brought with it something I'd never seen before—anger. "Anne Rose Shepard, what a simply horrible thing to say. John Cornwall is a nice man, a fine man. Any interest he has shown in the trunk has been because he cares about folks and their concerns. I never thought you'd say such a hurtful thing about someone."

"I'm...I'm sorry, Grandma Rose. I...."

"It's YOU who is obsessed about this trunk, not John Cornwall. And you need to do some thinking, young lady, about that key I mentioned earlier. Goodbye!"

I'd never seen Grandma Rose go off in such a huff. Of course, in years past I'd only had short visits with Grandma Rose. Now that we were living in the same town, we'd gotten to spend more time with each other. And the more time you spend with a person, the more you see their flip sides.

Oh, great, God, now Grandma Rose is mad at me too?

I slowly climbed the creaky stairs. There was something wrong with everything in the house—cracked walls, faded wallpaper, leaky pipes, uneven floors. A mess of a house.

A mess of a family, too, God?

I walked back up to my room and found that Maria and Alia had looked up the locksmith's number again.

"You call him," Alia was saying, pushing the phone toward Maria.

"No, you call him." Maria pushed the phone back to Alia.

"I'll call him," I said as I entered the room. "231-0204." I waited several rings, then the answering machine started up. It was the key-to-the-problem jingle again.

"Hi, this is Annie Shepard again. There's no lock number on the lock on the trunk. It just says American Lock Company. I guess we'll need to have you come take a look at it unless you have a generic American Lock Company key. My number is 231-0416. Thanks."

I hung up the phone. "So what now?"

"Dynamite the trunk?" Maria laughed.

"No," said Alia. "That's too drastic. Let's just chuck it over Annie's balcony."

I gave them a dumb look. They deserved it, even though I knew they were trying to cheer me up. I tried to think while they kept giving other brilliant ideas to open the trunk.

"Push it down the stairs."

"Try a bottle opener."

"Or a corkscrew."

"Put it in the back of Link's trunk. Maybe it will fall out in traffic and a truck will run over it and smash open the lock."

I'd had it. "Will you two stop? I'm trying to think. Work with me on this. I'm trying to think how we could reach the original owner of this house."

Maria scrunched up her face and sat down. "But the neon orange said she couldn't find the information."

Alia joined us on the floor. "I never believed that, did you, Annie? She must have all the names in a file somewhere."

"You're right. When you buy a house, you have to have all the names—that only makes sense. I think Esther Reel is keeping something from us. But if she is, where could we find it? Where would there be records of who owned this house?"

We looked at each other for a few moments. Then a light-bulb went on inside Maria.

"You're not going to like this, Annie," she said. "The museum?"

She was right. My stomach suddenly had a pit in it. "Ugh."

"She's right, Annie," said Alia. "They would have maps and things like that there."

"They also have John Cornwall there," I said. And then something occurred to me. Perhaps we could do a little fishing about John Cornwall as well as about the former house owner. "We could pretend to be thanking him about the keys and see how much he really knows about trunks, too. Maybe we could even hang around and follow him. See if his intentions with Grandma Rose are honest. See if there really are rodents in the museum."

Maria and Alia looked a little confused. I hadn't told them about all my suspicions. But I'd fill them in on the way. We could definitely kill two birds with one museum trip. Or at least one rat.

15

A NAME

Maria looked at her watch. "Four thirty. It's getting late."

I opened the museum door, backing in. "I know. We probably should have waited until tomorrow. Let's just get the information and get going. That way, maybe we won't have to run into old what's–his–name."

"Mr. Cornwall." Alia looked a little strange.

"Right," I said. "Cornwall—what's-his-name Cornwall."

"Right," said a man's voice behind me. "Only it's *John* Cornwall."

I gulped and turned around slowly. He held the door open as we inched into the museum and toward the gift counter.

"Oh, hello there, sir. Fancy meeting you here."

He smiled and his eye twitched again. "What a coincidence, Miss Shepard. I was just visiting with your mother."

"I know," I said. "I was in another room. How are your

rats?"

"Rats?" He smoothed back his white hair. "Oh, of course, you mean the mice here in the museum. Well, so far they're alive and well. Perhaps they won't be tomorrow, though. They're chewing through a lot of our books and papers." He paused. "But that's not why you're here, is it?"

"No," I said. "I've, uh, taken an, uh, interest in local history. Real local history. In fact, it's so local, it's, uh, my house."

Maria jumped in. "Yes, it's a fascinating old house, Mr. Cornwall, so fascinating, in fact, that...."

"I'd like to know who lived there before us," I finished.

"Do you have that type of information here?" asked Alia.

Mr. Cornwall patted his forefinger to his mouth in thought. "Well, we could probably dig it up somehow. But it would be much quicker to go across the street to the courthouse and look it up there."

"The courthouse?" I eyed him carefully, wondering if he were trying to get rid of us.

"Yes," he said. "All the offices are computerized. It should be easy for the assessor or the recorder to look that up. Have you ever been in the courthouse?"

Maria and Alia nodded, but I shook my head.

Mr. Cornwall looked around the museum for a moment. "Things are pretty dead here. I should be able to leave early." He walked over to the counter. "Dora! Dora?" Docent Dora came running from a back room. "Dora, I'm going to help these lovely ladies look up some information at the courthouse. Can you handle things here and lock up for me tonight?"

Docent Dora cleared her throat and wiped her hands on her white docent smock. "Why, certainly Mr. C. You just go on. I've got things completely under control.

Mr. Cornwall turned toward us. "Well, let's go, ladies. To the courthouse!"

My earlier suspicions of John Cornwall were evaporating. He seemed so nice and helpful now. If it weren't for the twitching eye, I might even like him. But there still was something holding me back from completely trusting him. Why would someone want to help some curious teenaged girls? It didn't make sense.

But he was right. It only took the assessor's clerk a couple minutes to look up the parcel number for our house. And then it only took a couple more minutes for the clerk in the recorder's office to run off a copy of the grant deed. As I paid the tall, friendly lady $2.50, she handed the paper to me. I wanted to read it right then and there but didn't feel comfortable with John Cornwall standing over us most curiously. I folded it up and put it in my jeans pocket.

"Uh, thank you, Mr. Cornwall," I said instead. "This will be most helpful for my research project."

"So now what?" he asked, instead of taking the hint to leave.

Why don't you get lost was what I wanted to say, but instead what came out was, "Well, I don't know—got any ideas?"

"Since you now have the name of the former owner or owners, you could go to the newspaper office to see if there's anything about those people in the morgue." He turned to go. "At least that's what I would do. I'm a very curious fellow, you could say. But I'm getting the idea you ladies are too. Aren't you?" He smiled again, his eye twitching once more. He didn't wait for an answer but instead waved and left.

"That guy is weird," said Maria. "I don't like the way he looks at us."

"Me either," said Alia. "He gives me the woolies."

"Willies," I corrected her. "But that is a good idea he gave us—to go to the newspaper."

"But why would he say to look in the morgue?" Alia asked. "Isn't a morgue where they keep dead people?"

"Yeah," said Maria. "That was weird. But maybe there's a connection there somehow. Maybe he knows something he's not telling us." She paused. "So, Annie, what's it say?"

I'd almost forgotten. I pulled out the deed from my jeans pocket and unfolded it, leading the other two out of the office and into the courthouse hallway. I held it out and read, "For valuable consideration, receipt of which is hereby acknowledged, Edward Tristan, trustee for the Estate of Sarah Millerton, hereby grants to Mark T. Shepard and Katherine Martoni Shepard, husband and wife as joint tenants, the real property..."

"I'm confused," said Alia. "Who is the former owner— the Edward guy or the Sarah lady?"

"Well," Maria said, "the neon orange said the trustee guy was the one who signed the papers for the former owner. So Sarah—what's her name..."

"...Millerton," I read again.

"So Sarah Millerton must be the former owner. At least that's what I'd guess." Maria shrugged her shoulders.

"Sarah Millerton." I smiled. "So Sarah Millerton is the owner of my trunk."

We turned around the corner for the side door of the courthouse where we had entered. But as we did I about dropped the deed, because there ahead of us in a phone booth with the door ajar was a man in a jogging suit—the same man who had stopped at our house the other night asking about a trunk. He was holding the receiver down, as though he'd been interrupted in his phone call. And the man he was talking to outside the phone booth was John Cornwall.

16

DEAD BURRITO

We didn't really have time to dwell on the connection between the two trunk hunters. It was five o'clock, the sun was setting, and each of us was pushing it timewise with our parents. I found that out as soon as I walked through the front door.

"You're dead meat."

That cheerful greeting was from my loving older brother Link who was clutching a microwaved packaged burrito. He had transformed to small mountain town living quickly and was wearing a jeans jacket over a plain white T-shirt that was tucked into unbelted faded jeans.

"Huh?"

"Annie, is that you?" Dad yelled from the kitchen. "I need to see you right here, right now."

"Told ya, Shorty," Link added as he strode upstairs, two steps at a time.

"What's the matter, Dad?" I pushed the swinging door into the kitchen. Burrito? I instantly remembered. Mom had told me before I left the feed store to be home early to throw together some supper.

"Didn't your mother mention that she and I have a meeting tonight?"

"Yeah, I...."

"And didn't she ask you to fix some dinner for the family?"

"Yeah, I...."

"And didn't she...."

I spaced out. It wasn't going to do any good to answer Dad until he was all done ranting. Which wasn't for a couple more minutes. Dad's ranting was more like calm interrogation—smooth and thorough. I took over at the microwave while he tore up some lettuce.

Mom and Dad were going to a Chamber of Commerce meeting. Mom was uptight, because she was a mess from working at the feed store. I understood. Working with feed all day doesn't exactly leave you with a terrific aroma.

Riiiiiinnnnnngggg. It was the doorbell. I wondered if Maria or Alia had left something here and started for the door.

"Oh, no you don't, young lady." Dad stepped in front of me. "I'll get it. You finish making dinner."

I started heating another burrito and then turned on the dish water. Dishes were still left from breakfast. Things were always a mess in the kitchen, it seemed, with the four of us going in all directions. I had things about under control and even a few plates set on the table when I heard a thunk-thunk-

thunk coming down the stairs.

After about the tenth thunk, I decided to peek out the kitchen door. Link was dragging my trunk down the stairs by the side leather handle. And standing at the front door was the man we'd seen at the courthouse in the phone booth.

I had to risk Dad's anger. "Dad?" I pushed open the kitchen door. "What's he...."

"Annie, this is the locksmith you apparently called. He's come to take the trunk back to his shop."

"But I...I didn't think he'd take the trunk away, Dad."

The man grabbed the other handle of the trunk and began carrying it toward the front door with Link on the other end.

"I thought he'd be able to unlock it right here."

The man set his end down. He scowled, which made his chiseled face even more angular. "You didn't say that when you called. I thought you wanted this done immediately. Your message sounded urgent, so I came right away."

Dad had on his dead-meat look again. "Anne, you should not make this type of arrangement for services without consulting your mother or me." He turned to the locksmith and got out his wallet. "I'm sorry for your trouble, sir. How much is your house call fee?"

The man grunted. "Well, normally fifty bucks. But I haven't done anything." He took a long look at the trunk. "Pretty nice trunk you've got there. I wouldn't mind having that myself. Are you interested in selling it?"

He looked at Dad. Dad looked at me. "No," I said. "It's beginning to have some sentimental attachment. Not until I can get it unlocked anyway and see what's...." I bit my lip. The last thing I wanted to do was get someone else interested in the trunk.

He scratched his head. "Well, I would take care of that lock right now, but I don't have my tools with me. Don't worry about a fee—just forget it."

Dad got out a ten-dollar bill. "Please take this for your time. I guess we'll get back to you about the trunk. I'm sorry for the confusion." He shot me the dead-meat look again for my benefit.

The man took the ten dollar-bill. "Well, thanks anyway."

I stared after him as he jogged down the front steps. There was something about his voice—the way he said, "Well, thanks anyway"—that sounded familiar. I shook it off. I was sure getting silly, thinking that everything in life was a doo-doo doo-doo sort of thing.

"Mark, who was that?" Mom was putting on her earrings as she descended the stairs.

"Long story, dear. I'll tell you later."

"He looked familiar." She shook her head and turned toward me. "Annie, is dinner ready?"

"Yes, Mom, all set. Burritos and salad." I backtracked to the kitchen.

"Sounds wonderful," Mom deadpanned. "Just what I need before a Chamber of Commerce meeting, huh, Mark?"

I ate in silence. Mom and Dad semi-argued about feed store bills. Link popped in and out of the room, picking up something new to eat on each visit. Attached to his ear was the portable phone, presumably with Crystal on the other end.

Mom and Dad left in a huff, hardly saying a word to each other or to me. Dad suggested that Link could take the trunk back upstairs as they opened the front door.

"Dad! No way! Let Annie do it. It's her trunk. She's the one who called the locksmith. I was the one who was nice enough to bring it downstairs for her. I'm definitely not nice enough to take it back up, though. It's her problem. Let her do it."

Dad gritted his teeth as he started to close the door. "Thank you both for your cooperative attitudes today. It really makes your mother and me feel great." He smirked and left.

Link turned to me. "It's your trunk. It's your problem. YOU take it back upstairs. I have better things to do."

I wanted to say something back but had run out of sarcasm. I tried tugging on the trunk. If it were smaller, I could probably lift it, but its bulk kept me from budging it. I kicked the lock. Stupid thing.

"You caused this whole big mess," I said to the trunk. "Where is your key?"

What was the key, Grandma Rose had talked about? "The fear of the Lord is the key to this treasure?" I don't get it. God, how could fearing You be a key?

17

BAD NEWS, GOOD NEWS, BAD NEWS

It was another one of those wet pillow nights. The kind when you start out crying about everything and end up wondering why you're crying at all 'cause it doesn't do any good. Mom and Dad came home after I was on my third pillow. A few minutes later, Dad peeked into my room and whispered, "Annie," but I pretended I was sleeping. I was just tired of all the fighting and everything.

He came in and closed my pre-algebra book that was about falling off my bed. I'd gotten stuck on negative exponents and that's when the crying started. I felt as if I were a negative to the millionth power. It just seemed as though nothing in my life was falling into place. Dad sighed. He pulled my blanket up over my ear the way I like it and stood there for a moment. I thought about saying something but didn't.

I woke up to the weirdest smell Wednesday morning:

Breakfast. I sniffed. Bacon? I sniffed again. French toast? Was I in the right house? I looked around the room. Yup, it was mine. And breakfast was definitely a reason to get up. A few minutes later I was combing my wet hair as I ran down the stairs. I pushed open the kitchen door to find both Mom and Dad at the stove.

"Morning, Annie," Mom and Dad said at once.

"Morning." I sat down and grabbed a piece of bacon, biting into it. "You guys must have had a good meeting last night, huh?"

"It was fine," Mom said.

"We made a great contact for the feed store," Dad said. "A good hay source." He smiled. "So, how'd things go here last night?"

"Okay, I guess." I grabbed a piece of French toast. "Link was his usual cooperative self."

Dad turned around, puzzled. "But I see he took your trunk upstairs."

I looked up. "No, he didn't, Dad. It's still...." I paused. Had I seen it when I came downstairs?

"It's not there," Dad said. "He must have."

I picked up another piece of bacon and walked back into the entry hall. No trunk. I looked around the living room and then the dining room. No trunk. *Maybe he put it in my room while I was sleeping*. I ran up the stairs and back around the short hall to my room. I turned on the light and stood there a moment. No trunk.

I pounded on the bathroom door. The shower was going.

"Link!" I pounded again. "Link!"

"What?"

The shower stopped.

"What did you do with my trunk?"

"Your trunk again? Is that why you disturbed my shower?" The shower started again. "Nothing, Shorty. Now leave me alone."

I fumed downstairs. Link had done nothing with it. And then I stopped halfway. He'd done nothing with it? Then where was it?

"Dad!" I ran the rest of the way downstairs. "Mom! Dad! My trunk's been stolen!"

Mom and Dad came rushing out of the kitchen.

"It's not in your room?" Mom asked.

"Link didn't put it somewhere?" Dad said.

I shook my head. "It's gone! It was right here when I went to bed last night."

Mom walked over to the front door and tried the door handle. It was unlocked. "Mark, did you get the newspaper yet?"

Dad shook his head. "No. You usually do."

"Then you forgot to lock the door." Mom shut the door. "I asked you to lock the door last night."

"I thought I did," Dad said.

Mom was turning red. "No, Mark, you didn't. And now it looks like someone came in here sometime during the night and stole the trunk. Is anything else gone?"

Mom and Dad proceeded to check the rest of the house. Nothing else was missing or disturbed. Dad called the sheriff's department and arranged to have a report taken while he was at the feed store later. Then my parents went off to the feed store—in separate cars. Link flew off in his truck. I locked the front door and headed off to meet Maria and Alia before school.

"You're kidding," they said together as I told them about the theft.

"Nope."

"That's terrible," said Alia.

"No, that's terrific," said Maria.

"Why?" I swung my backpack to my left side.

"No one would steal the trunk unless it was worth something," said Maria. "Either there's something valuable in it, or the trunk itself is worth a lot."

"Yeah," I said, "we've just got to find it now. But, come to think of it, there are only a few people who even know about the trunk."

"Esther Reel," said Maria.

"John Cornwall," said Alia.

"And the locksmith," I said. "Did I tell you he stopped by last night and was going to take it away?"

"You're kidding," said Maria.

"No, and he said he wanted it for himself—or something like that." I swung my backpack to my right shoulder.

"Doo-doo doo-doo, doo-doo doo-doo," sung Maria.

"What?" I stopped in my tracks.

"A locksmith?" said Maria. "Maybe the house *was* locked. Maybe someone—someone who can unlock locks like a locksmith—opened it in the night and took the trunk."

"Doo-doo doo-doo, doo-doo doo-doo," sung Alia.

"What?" I stopped again.

"Esther Reel," said Alia. "It was just yesterday we found her snooping around your house, Annie. We saw her try the back door handle. Maybe your dad really did lock the door. Real estate people have a way of getting into houses. They have lots of keys. And she was interested in the trunk too. She knows about the lost Mountain City fortune."

"That's true." I sighed. Then I had a thought. "Or could it be...."

"Who?" the other two interrupted.

"John Cornwall. I still don't trust him. You should be able to look someone in the eye. He has that twitchy eye. There's something about him that seems secretive. And we know he knows about the trunk too." I paused.

"So what do we do?" Alia asked.

"Each of us could go visit a different person after school and snoop around a little," said Maria.

"I d-d-don't...." Alia's voice got squeaky.

"That's not safe," I said. "Let's just start with the closest person—Esther Reel—then stop by the museum, then try the locksmith's place. Two of us could distract the person while the other one snoops around."

"Cool," said Maria. "Real cloak-and-dagger stuff."

"Clock and dagger? I don't have a clock," said Alia. "And I definitely don't have a dagger."

I looked at Maria and Maria looked at me. Somehow we knew that Alia would not be the one doing the snooping.

18

STILL ANOTHER TRUNK HUNTER

After school we found ourselves hustling to Reel Real Estate. On the way we stopped by the feed store so I could let Mom know I'd be gone for the afternoon.

"Doing what, exactly?" Mom was semi-busy with a customer who couldn't make up his mind.

"Umm, research," I said.

"For a project," Maria added quickly.

"An *important* project," Alia said.

Mom walked to the cash register; the customer had finally decided. "Okay, but do the cages first, Annie."

Ugh. My face fell. I didn't have time to do the cages. I turned around apologetically to Maria and Alia and was ready to suggest that they head off without me when Maria and Alia did the strangest but nicest thing. Maria set down her backpack. And then Alia set down hers. Maria walked over to the first cage and pulled out the tray with shavings. Alia then walked over to the next cage and did the same thing. Then they both took them over to the trash and dumped them, turning around and smiling at me like they'd just won the Olympics or something.

"What are you guys doing?" I set down my backpack.

"Helping you, silly," said Alia.

"Yeah," said Maria, "we're the After School Sleuths, and that makes us family. And family sticks together—through thick or thin."

"And even through shavings and animal droppings." Alia stuck out her tongue and pretended to swoon.

I looked at my two pathetic, wonderful friends. It was true. They were becoming like family to me. And even if my real family were falling apart, I knew I still had my new best friends.

We made quick work of the cleaning cages event. In fact, I figured it was a new record—seven minutes and some seconds. When I started humming the Olympics theme song, Maria and Alia laughed. And then they joined in on the humming as we grabbed our backpacks and headed for the door, raising our arms together as though we were on the victory stand. Mom laughed and shook her head as we headed out the door, bumping together like the Three Stooges.

Since Esther Reel's office was just a couple blocks away, we made it in just a few minutes. The tiny one-story frame house was one in a row of what had been mill houses. In the earlier part of the century, the sawmill provided housing for its employees. Now the buildings served as businesses— a barbershop, a pet grooming place, a florist, and others.

Esther's office was on the corner, surrounded by a tall green hedge. I looked around warily to make sure I didn't bump into Esther again.

We tiptoed to the back corner edge to see what the back entrance looked like. There was a back door and small overhang covering the one-step-up stoop. Esther's bicycle rested against the stoop.

"I could try and sneak in the back door while you guys distract her in the front office." I bit my lip. It looked kind of scary now that it was right in front of me. And I wasn't sure about sneaking into someone's property. I felt a sudden queasiness. "I have to go to the bathroom."

"Perfect!" said Maria.

"Huh?"

"Just follow me." Maria pulled on my sweatshirt sleeve. "You have to go to the bathroom. I'm sure Esther has a bathroom.... Got it?"

I smiled. I'd gotten it. Now if I could just hold it.

A bell tinkled as we opened the front door. A fat orange cat sitting in a sunny front window meowed and then closed its eyes again, hunching back into position. The neon orange suddenly appeared in the front room which obviously had been the living room in the house. She matched the decor, which looked like 1960s leftovers—four molded orange plastic chairs facing a large desk with a faded turquoise top.

"Faded" matched the neon orange because the smile on her face faded as she noticed who we were. She instantly, however, put a fake one back into place. "Nice to see you angels," she said through her teeth. "How can I help you?"

I danced in place on my tiptoes. "Mrs. Reel, could I use your bathroom? I really need to...." I wasn't lying. I did.

"Gee whiz, is that all? Why, certainly. It's just down that short hall—right next to my personal office."

I grinned like she was. Personal office? That was just what I was hoping to find. After I found the bathroom, I peeked into Esther's office. Papers were stacked in files high on her desk. Several file cabinets faced inward from the side walls. Where would I start looking? But just as I started into the room, I overheard Esther talking to Maria and Alia.

"It's such a coincidence that you girls dropped by today. I talked yesterday to the trustee of the estate that used to own the Shepard house. He's in the area vacationing. I told him about that trunk you girls found. He wants to see it while he's here."

I tiptoed back down toward the front room.

"See it?" Maria said.

"The trunk?" Alia said.

I gritted my teeth. I hoped Maria and Alia wouldn't tell the neon orange that the trunk had been stolen.

"Why, yes," said Esther Reel. "Would that be a problem?"

"Well...." said Maria.

I stepped into the room. "Would what be a problem, Mrs. Reel?"

"Oh, my goodness, Miss Shepard. I was just telling your friends that the trustee for the former owner would like to see your trunk. He didn't say whether or not he wanted it—he'd just like to see it. He'll be calling back to confirm a seven o'clock appointment. Would that be convenient?"

I nodded. Seven? Tonight? What would I do if we couldn't find the trunk?

I bit the sides of my mouth. I looked up at the ceiling. I needed inspiration. I needed an excuse. Oh, shucks! I needed...to tell the truth.

"Mrs. Reel, a terrible thing has happened."

Maria and Alia looked cross-eyed at me.

"The trunk has been stolen."

"Stolen!" Esther swayed backwards, and for a moment I thought she was going to either pass out or puke. She rested on the edge of the turquoise desk.

Alia and I reached over to steady the opposite sides of her. I watched her eyes to make sure her reaction was genuine.

"Yes, it's terrible," I said. "Someone broke into our house last night and took it."

Esther looked up and looked down and then took a deep breath. "Did you report this to the sheriff's office?" she whispered.

I looked around. Why she was whispering? "No."

She sighed in relief.

"My parents did."

She gulped. "Oh, my goodness. Now there'll be a mess. Just a mess. A very big mess."

I looked at her carefully. "You mean with the trustee?"

She patted her chest. "Why, umm, yes, of course. What else, umm, could I mean? It's that man. He's very..." She paused. "...demanding."

"Demanding?" I asked.

"Demanding. He wants.... He has to...." She looked at me.

It seemed as though she were afraid of the man.

"Mrs. Reel," said Alia, "he doesn't sound very nice. Are you afraid of....What did you say his name was?"

"Tristan," said Esther. "Edward Tristan. He's not a very pleasant man to deal with. I don't look forward to telling him about the trunk being stolen."

"Well, I'm sorry," I said. "I'm sure the sheriff's department is working on the case. Maybe they'll find that trunk. Maybe even the lost Mountain Center fortune is in it, and...and...we all could share it and live happily ever after." For some reason I felt I needed to cheer up the neon orange.

She smiled, for real this time. "Oh, I doubt that. Edward Tristan would not allow that. He's a very difficult man. You'll see...."

"We'll see?" I asked.

"Yes, you'll see. Because he's going to visit your home tonight."

19

SNOOPING JOHN C.

"I don't think Esther Reel took the trunk." Maria was setting a brisk pace to the museum.

"I agree," said Alia, almost running to keep up with Maria. "She genuinely seemed surprised about the trunk being gone."

"I don't know," I said. "She seemed nervous, like she had something to hide." I paused. "And I just thought of something. She never mentioned whether she checked the file about our house. Remember? I had asked her who would legally own the trunk—my family or the former owner, and she said she would check the file."

"That's right," said Alia. "She never mentioned that, although she did say she'd talked to the trustee, which meant she must have looked into the file."

"Maybe...." Maria slowed a step. "...maybe she knows that

your family owns the trunk legally and isn't telling you so that she can try and weasel it away."

I laughed. "Well, no one can weasel it away now, since it's already been weaseled away."

A quick half-mile later and we were downtown and heading up the walk to the museum. But just as we were walking up the steps, John Cornwall rushed out the door.

"Well, hello, girls. Interesting that I just happened to bump into you. I was just reading up on trunks. From the description your grandmother gave me, Annie, it seems your trunk was fairly common for folk in this area in the early part of the century. It's certainly interesting, finding a trunk like that in an attic, but probably not of much value other than what you'd get from an antique dealer." He smiled. "Or me. I'd be interested in it, since I restore trunks as a hobby." His left eye twitched. "Could I drop by, perhaps this evening, to see it?"

I looked at Maria and Alia, and they looked at me. Didn't we just have this conversation?

"Mr. Cornwall, the fact is...the trunk was stolen last night."

"Stolen?" His left eye twitched again.

"Yes, stolen. And my parents have reported it to the police. So, I guess that takes care of that."

"Did you ever find out any more information about the former owner, umm, what was her name...Sarah Millerton?" John Cornwall took my elbow firmly and walked me down the stairs.

I looked at this man. Why was he so interested in all of this? What was he trying to find out? Did he really care or was he trying to distract me from finding out something about him? Or was it even possible he didn't want me to go into the museum?

"No," I said. "We have some other research we're working on today, Mr. Cornwall."

"Well, this won't take but a few minutes. Let me take you over to *The Mountain Center Messenger* office, and they'll find something for you in the morgue."

The morgue? I looked at Maria and Alia. Their faces probably reflected mine—sheer white fright. I pulled away from John Cornwall's grasp and stood between Maria and Alia facing him. There was no way he was going to lead us to some morgue. I took a hard look at the man. He wore a gray, V-necked sweater over a white turtleneck shirt and dark gray, cotton slacks. His black loafers were spitshine perfect. He seemed sort of nice, but I'd heard that the most deranged criminals appeared at first to be friendly and kind. And there was that twitching eye.

He stared at us for a moment and then all of a sudden he laughed. "Oh, my heavens. It just occurred to me that you've never heard of that term before—morgue. Do you know what a morgue is?"

Alia squeaked. "Where they put dead people?"

I looked at her. I couldn't believe it. Alia had gotten it right.

He laughed again, doubling over. "Well, of course you're right. But a newspaper has one too. A newspaper morgue is where they keep all the old newspapers. Articles are arranged in files by subject, so you can, for example, look up all the articles *The Messenger* has ever printed on gold mining and quickly have them right in front of you. Some papers do it with files. This paper has microfilm. Some larger papers have it all computerized. It's a pretty handy deal."

When I picked up my jaw from the floor, I cleared my throat, and felt my neck and face regain color. At that point I was so surprised and speechless that I let John Cornwall lead us to the newspaper office which was just on the other side of the courthouse building. There he introduced us to the news editor, Maggie Lewis, who was winding down for the day.

"Call me Maggie," she said right away, holding out her hand to each of us and squeezing firmly. She was about my height and wore a navy business jacket and slim skirt. She brushed back her shoulder-length hair and stuck her pencil behind her right ear. "Budding news reporters?"

"Maybe," I said. "I kind of like to write. But today we're interested in old news not new news."

"Well, we've got old news around here too," said Mrs. Lewis. "*The Messenger* is the oldest paper in California—we're having our one hundred and twenty-fifth anniversary next year. Just follow me."

She beckoned us through the newsroom. John Cornwall waved goodbye, and the rest of us walked around a series of desks grouped in sections. One section, she said was for news writers, one for the sports writers, one for the copyeditor, one for the feature writer. On each desk was a computer. All of them, she said, were networked with each other. A woman sat at one of the news desks, flipping through a thick book.

We followed her down a short hallway behind the newsroom.

"Here's the morgue," she said. She pointed into a small room the size of a big closet. In it were a couple of tables, bare except that a boxy machine sat on one of them. In a corner stood several file cabinets with small drawers. She stepped over to the file. "Exactly what kind of old news were you interested in?"

I walked into the room, and Maria and Alia followed me. "We're interested in a woman who lived in Mountain Center earlier in this century. Her name was Sarah Millerton. I'm sorry—that's all I know about her, except that I think she used to live in my house."

Mrs. Lewis raised her brows which made her brown wireframed glasses slip down her nose a little. "Sounds interesting—a little sleuthing, huh?" She sat down at the computer.

Alia looked real wide-eyed. "How'd you know?"

Maria cleared her voice. "You could just say we're curious about local history. Annie lives in an old house."

Good cover. Mrs. Lewis shrugged her shoulders and fingered through the file. She grabbed the pencil from her ear and wrote some dates on a sticky note she pulled from her pocket. Then she pulled out a film from another file and inserted it into the boxy machine and sat at the chair. A picture of an old newspaper appeared on the screen, and then page after page swished by as she turned the dial in front.

Soon it slowed and she squinted at the screen. "There it is—July 29, 1921."

We crowded around behind her as she read the headline and article aloud: "Twins born. Boy and girl twins were born to Sarah Millerton of Mountain Center, July 23. The boy, Charles William, is a healthy, strapping young man, but the girl died stillborn. Her mother named her Anne Leah, and she was laid to rest at the home on Tuesday. The babies were born about a month early, the mother having been bedridden for several months at her home at the foot of Forest Hill. There still has been no word of the father, Albert Millerton, who disappeared mysteriously in March. Some folk say he was shirking his fatherly responsibility, but others say he may have been hurt in a mining accident. No one knows for sure."

I stared at the screen…and gulped. Buried at the home? Could there be a mini-cemetery right in my backyard? With the remains of Sarah Millerton's baby girl? I looked at Maria and Alia. They had that whitish look on their faces again. We really were in a morgue!

20

MISTAKEN LOCATION

"Looks like you've got a wild story there, Annie," said Maggie Lewis. "Mysterious disappearance…grave of a still-born baby….Sounds like something I'd like to dig into."

Dig into? I looked at her sideways. And then she smiled and laughed. A joke. I half-laughed and then Maria and Alia followed suit.

"Hey, Maggie!" It was the woman calling from across the newsroom. "I got the address for that suspect's family."

"Great," said Maggie Lewis. "Did you find it in the City Directory?"

"Yeah," said the woman. "Thanks for the tip—it was there. I'm going to run over to this place and see if they'll give me an interview."

Maggie Lewis turned back to us. "Handy book, that City Directory is. If you know a phone number, but not an address, you can look it up in the City Directory. It's like a reverse phone book."

That gave me an idea. "Maggie, do you think I could use that book? We're trying to...."

She smiled. "More sleuthing?"

I nodded.

"Anything to help a budding reporter. But only if you promise to write this Sarah Millerton story up for me when you get it all put together. Okay?"

"Why, umm, sure. When things open up for us, I'll write it all up for you." I looked at Maria and Alia. They smiled back. They'd gotten my private joke.

Maggie brought the City Directory over to us at the front counter and said goodbye. I dug the locksmith's phone number out of my jeans pocket and unfolded it. 231-0204. I looked it up. "Here it is—241 Main Street. Cool. That's just two blocks down, isn't it?"

"Hmm..." said Maria, "...241 Main? That sounds familiar for some reason."

As I thought about it, it kind of rang a bell with me too, but I couldn't place it either. We waved goodbye to Maggie and headed out the front glass doors. It was a few minutes after four, and so we didn't dawdle past the theater posters or the bakery, our usual loitering spots.

"I don't think it's John Cornwall, either," said Maria.

"Yeah," said Alia. "He's been so helpful these past two days. He took us to the courthouse and today to the newspaper office. He's going out of his way to be nice. Why should he do that?"

"To get the trunk," I said. "I don't know exactly what it is—his shifty eye or what—but I don't trust him."

"I know why," said Maria.

"Why?" I shifted my backpack again.

"You don't like it that your Grandma Rose is dating a man. She's got a life now, and you're jealous 'cause she's not spending the time with you. And so you're taking it out on John Cornwall."

"That's not true. I haven't even had time to see Grandma Rose—how can I be jealous of time he's taking up?"

"I don't know," said Maria. "It just seems like you're a little on the rude side with him."

"Rude? Me, rude? Thank you very much, Maria Martinez."

We walked in semi-silence the rest of the way to 241 Main Street. It was semi-silence, because Alia was humming. It wasn't country music this time. It was stuff like "Jesus Loves Me" and "Amazing Grace" and some others I wasn't too sure of but had heard on the radio on Sunday morning. I figured that was better than "Stand by Your Man." In fact, I decided that if Maria and Alia started singing that one together, I was going to punch 'em. Maybe.

It just seemed like everything was a confusing mess. And as we stood in front of 241 Main Street, we were even more confused. That was because 241 Main Street was not the location for the locksmith, but the location for an antiques store. Glass windows on either side of the recessed door displayed all kinds of old things. A drop-leaf table held a teapot decorated in a tiny floral print. Next to it were several teacups and feminine things—lacy gloves, a black velvet hat with a peacock's plume at a tilt, a pink-tinted perfume bottle. On the other side was a mixture of clunkier items—jugs, washboards, a big copper container with handles. Furniture was arranged everywhere—a maze of old things. A tall man with dark hair looked up from a counter that stood out from the right wall.

"This looks interesting," said Alia. "I love old stuff."

"Yeah, but it's not the locksmith's." Maria stood back from the building and looked up and down the street. "There's no shop on this block that says anything about a locksmith." She looked up. "Hey, this is Mountain Center Antiques. Wasn't that the ad we read in the paper? They were looking for trunks."

"That's right," I said. "Well, we could go inside and see what our trunk *might* have been worth."

Just then a bell jingled. The man who had been working behind the side counter opened the door. And at the very moment he opened his mouth, I realized three things all at once. He was the locksmith who had come to the house about my trunk. He was wearing the same black hooded jogging suit as the man who had jogged to my house and...the locksmith *was* the jogger who was the antique dealer. And he was standing right in front of me.

"Did you decide you wanted that trunk opened after all?"

I looked at him a little weakly. It wasn't a how-do-you-do-can-I-help-you kind of question at all. It was more like a why-are-you-here kind of question. And I was feeling a little queasy in my stomach. Could this man have stolen my trunk?

Did he have it in his shop right at that moment? Did he open it and find the lost Mountain Center fortune?

He certainly didn't seem too inviting, standing there filling the doorway with his arms crossed and his weight boxed squarely on two spread feet. A five o'clock shadow covered his chiseled jaw, and his deepset, green eyes glared at me without a blink.

"Umm, no sir, we were just interested in your lovely gift items here in the window. We thought we'd look around a little, if you don't mind." I gave him a Pollyanna smile.

He looked at us suspiciously, then stepped back a little, opening the door for us. "Well, okay. I usually don't let in more than two teenagers at a time, but you ladies look harmless. By the way, I'm George Harris." He forced a broad smile, revealing a gold crown on one of his back teeth.

I gulped. Harmless? Would it be safe for us in there together? I looked at Maria and Alia and cleared my throat. "Maria, Alia, you know what kind of thing I'm looking for." I gave them *The Look*. "Why don't you look that way, Maria, and Alia, why don't you go that way? That way we won't have to take too long."

The man frowned. *Dumb me*, I thought. *That's a typical teen technique for shoplifting—divide and conquer. He probably thinks we're going to take something. I just wanted us to spread quickly, in case he was going to jump us. It'd be harder if we went in different directions.*

What was that sound? I looked over at Alia. Yup. She was humming "Amazing Grace" again, with sort of a country soul twang. Loudly. What a nicely weird friend.

I looked over at the man. He smiled and shook his head. I guess he hadn't had too many teenagers in his shop humming "Amazing Grace." He walked back to the counter and began working again on his record book.

Maria, Alia, and I zigzagged through the maze of old tables, chairs, and other furniture that displayed an array of anything and everything. My eyes riveted to every trunk in my path. There were several—one was even painted pink—but not one was mine. I kept an eye out for Maria and Alia as I wandered to the back of the store and then to the front again. When we met at the front door, I knew what they would say.

"I didn't find it," said Maria.

"Me either." Alia put her arm on my shoulder. "I'm sorry. I thought that maybe God was leading us here—it being a strange coincidence and all. You know what I mean?"

"I know," I whispered. The man was still working on his books. "I had the same thought. But, oh well."

Maria reached for the door handle and pulled it open. The bell tinkled again. The man looked up. No smile.

"Still," Maria said, "it is eerie that the locksmith and the antique dealer are the same man. Who better to know the value of something old than an antique dealer?"

Alia walked through the door and turned back. Under her breath she said, "And who better to know how to get into a house than a locksmith."

Maria and I walked through the door and I pulled it shut. "Maybe you guys are right. Maybe he did steal the trunk. And I guess I was pretty silly to think he'd have it right here for the whole world to see in his shop. Duh. He probably got rid of it somehow. Even if someone else tried to unload it, the police would look here first. Duh. Guys, I think I'm out of brains. I need a refill."

Maria and Alia agreed and we knew without saying where we were headed: Grandma Rose's house. Besides, I wanted to give her the third degree about John Cornwall. I still couldn't eliminate him from my lineup.

21

STANDING
BY THE MAN

We knew we wouldn't be able to stay long at Grandma Rose's. It was four thirty. But it didn't take long to walk the two blocks behind the museum to her rose-vine-covered cottage. I figured she'd have a pot of soup simmering, since it was family night at the church, and I knew she'd be going.

Sometimes she had my family over for a bite to eat on Wednesdays, then tried to get us all to go with her. But we never had. Mom and Dad had fallen away from church-going after they'd gotten married and involved in work and social circles in L.A. And since they started the feed store business, it seemed as though they didn't have time for God stuff. Sunday mornings were often spent picking up hay somewhere and sweeping up the small attached warehouse behind the store where all the feed was stored.

When Grandma Rose opened the door, I knew I was right.

Soup or something was on the stove. There she stood with her rose-print apron and a wooden spoon in her hand.

"Well, come on in, ladies, I've got some hot wheat-germ muffins right out of the oven."

Grandma Rose was a health nut. While things often smelled good at her house, digesting them was another matter. Some of her baked goods looked like they could have been made with feed store findings. But we found that with a smothering of butter and honey, the muffins went down quickly. In between bites I told Grandma Rose about the trunk and the leads we'd been following.

She poured hot water into our teacups. "And you say you found the name of the former owner of the house? I've always wondered. It's been boarded up for a long time. Why, before you and your family moved in, people forgot the house was even there—the trees and shrubbery were so over-grown."

I stirred my teabag. "Yes, Gram, the woman's name was Sarah Millerton. She...."

"Sarah Millerton?" Grandma Rose about dropped her kettle. "I know a Sarah Millerton. She lives at the convalescent hospital—she's been there forever, it seems."

I sipped my tea. "Yes, it seems she had two children—Charles William and Anne Leah. The girl died and...."

"And she's buried right at Annie's house," Alia interrupted. "Can you believe that? A grave right in her backyard some-where!"

"Oh, my heavens, this is becoming an interesting story." Grandma Rose took off her apron and sat down with us at her round table.

"That's what Maggie Lewis said at the newspaper office," I said. "She says she wants me to write a story for her when I have all the details figured out."

"Wonderful!" said Grandma Rose. "And I can help you. I was going to visit the convalescent patients tomorrow afternoon. Why don't you girls go with me? I can introduce you to Sarah Millerton."

"Wow!" said Maria. "At least we could learn what was in the trunk even if we don't ever get it back."

Grandma Rose sipped her tea, then set the cup down. "Well, it's not going to be that easy, Maria. You see, she has Alzheimer's disease, and she doesn't remember a lot. It's a debilitating disease of the mind—you progressively lose more and more of your memory."

"That is so sad," said Alia. "Does she know her son?"

"It's funny about the son," said Grandma Rose. "If he's still alive, I don't think he's ever visited. At least I've never heard of her having any visitors other than me or other church ladies who regularly visit the folks there. We'll ask her about him and see what she says."

She stood up. "Well, girls, I hate to scoot you out again, but I'm going to give you a quick ride home, because I've got company for dinner."

"My family?" I reached for my backpack.

"Not this time, dear. I've invited John over for some soup before family night at church."

I looked over at her in disgust. "Grandma Rose, are you sure about this thing with John Cornwall. He just doesn't....I don't....I can't seem to...."

She grabbed her handbag. "Just be honest, Anne Rose. You are your grandmother's granddaughter, after all."

"I...I'm not sure I trust the man, Grandma Rose." I shuffled my feet and stared at her tile floor.

"And why?"

Grandma Rose put on her coat, crossed her arms and cocked her head. She didn't look perturbed. Perhaps peeved. Maybe even provoked. But not perturbed...yet.

"I...I don't know. He...his eye twitches." I looked up at her weakly. I knew I didn't have a strong case.

"Anne Rose Shepard, m'thinks, to quote Shakespeare in *Othello*, 'thy honesty and love doth mince this matter.'"

"Huh?"

"You're not being objective because it's me, and you love me, and you're used to having me all to yourself."

Maria nodded. Alia said, "We told her that."

"John had a stroke a year or so ago, and his left side is still a little weak. He can't help that eye twitching. He's a kind, thoughtful man, Annie. Give him a chance, why don't you? You may learn to like him as much as I'm beginning to."

I sighed. "Boy, am I stupid."

She laughed. "No, you're not. You just love me and want to protect me. I think that's quite sweet, actually." She put her arms out to me, and I melted into them for one of her famous soft hugs.

"I don't want to lose you, Grandma Rose," I whispered. "You're about all I've got lately." A tear slid down onto her cotton dress.

She patted my head. "You'll never lose me, Anne Rose. Why, you could even gain a new grandpa out of this one."

Then she laughed.

I stood out at arms' length. "Why, Grandma Rose, is that for real?" I wiped my eyes.

She smiled impishly. "No, dear. Just a hunch. We'll see...."

We'll see? That was the famous family expression. "We'll see" was as good as a stamp of approval in my family. If you could get a "we'll see" out of Mom, Dad, or Grandma Rose, you could just about plan on it.

"Just you wait until you get to know John. He is the most interesting man I've met—other than your Grandpa Geno, of course. He's had a hard life, too. His mother abandoned him when he was young, and he bounced around a lot as a child." She smiled. "Just give him a chance, dear, won't you?"

I smiled back and gave her another hug. "Of course, Gram. You're the best. I should have known you'd pick the best."

I opened the front door and let Maria and Alia out. I paused for a second.

"I'm going to church tonight, Gram."

"Bringing your mom and dad and Lincoln with you?"

I grinned at her. Grandma Rose would never give up hope that her family would all go to church with her some day. I thought about that for a moment. Well, she had one down—three to go.

"I'll ask them, Gram. Gonna bring some of those wheat-germ muffins with you?"

"My goodness, no. I don't think there'll be enough left."

I laughed right out loud—so loud, in fact, that Maria and Alia turned around and looked, puzzled.

"Good, Grandma Rose. Good."

22

ANOTHER DISCOVERY

As soon as I entered the front door, I knew it was MPS: Moody Parents Syndrome.

"Is that you, Annie?" Mom was calling from the kitchen.

"Yeah, Mom."

"Your father and I need to see you."

I set my backpack down on the third stair of the stairway and pushed the swinging door into the kitchen.

"Have a seat, Annie." Uh-oh. Dad meant business. I sat down on one of the stools at the work station in the middle of the kitchen.

"We just got a strange phone call. The former owner of the house called and...."

"Former owner?" I couldn't believe Sarah Millerton had called—Gram had thought she was in her nineties.

"Well, not exactly....He was the trustee for the owner's

estate. His name is, let's see, I wrote it down...Edward Tristan. It seems Esther Reel called him about the trunk. Did you tell her about it?"

"Well, yes...I...."

"I thought so. Anyway, he's made a big stink about the whole thing and wants the trunk."

"Well, it's gone—did you tell him that?"

Mom turned from the stove. "Annie, the whole thing isn't any of his business, really. You see, I checked our contract of sale, and there was a finders-keepers clause in it. That means that any personal property left in the house is ours."

"And what did he say?"

Dad pulled on his chin like he does when he's annoyed. "He says he had no knowledge of a trunk left in the house, and that he wouldn't have signed the contract if he had known. He says if we don't turn it over, he's going to sue us."

I stood up. "Dad, that's not fair. And besides, the trunk is gone."

"True, but he could end up collecting anyway—from our insurance company. It's just that your mother and I don't want to make trouble. This is a small town. Word gets around quickly. We could become known as troublemakers. We could lose business if people lose faith in us. Do you understand?"

I looked at him. I didn't, really. I mean, what did I have to do with any of this? It wasn't my fault I found a trunk. It wasn't my fault it was stolen. I thought a minute. It *was* my fault that I opened my big mouth to Esther Reel. But I was just trying to be a good neighbor to find the real owners of the trunk. If it were theirs, I would have turned it over. But with the finders-keepers clause, it didn't seem right that someone should try and take it away. It was time to spill the beans to Mom and Dad.

"Dad, I bet Mrs. Reel told him about the lost Mountain Center fortune."

"The what?!" Mom turned around again.

I told them the whole story about the miner and his true love and their families disagreeing. But I didn't tell them the whole story about Maria and Alia and I looking all over town for information about the trunk and Sarah Millerton. When I finished, they were both smirking.

"Sweetie, that's a nice little story, but it sounds a little far-fetched to me." Mom patted me on my shoulder. I stood it for a moment, then moved away.

"Yes, dear, the likelihood of a trunk like that still existing and even being hidden away in our attic…a little unbelievable, don't you think?" Dad was trying to suppress an outright grin.

I looked at them. I hated being made fun of. I was thirteen years old—old enough to be taken seriously.

"Okay, whatever, so what do you want me to do?"

Dad had his serious look back. "Stay out of it, Annie. This guy seems nasty. Your mother and I will take care of it. Do you understand?"

I understood. Mom and Dad were messing with my life again. Telling me what to do. Not trusting me to make the right decisions for myself. Treating me like a kid. I turned away and started for the door. "Yeah, I understand," I said sarcastically.

"Excuse me, Annie? You're talking to your father."

I turned around. "Yes, Dad, I understand."

"That's better," said Mom. "Now go pick up your room—it's a mess. As soon as Link comes home from closing up the store, we'll sit down to dinner."

The front door opened.

"I think that's him now," Dad said.

As I pushed the kitchen door open, Link looked up as he was heading up the stairs. Just at that moment, he tripped over my backpack, twisting. He tried to catch himself, but he was carrying several notebooks and thick textbooks, and instead completely lost his footing and the books and landed on his back. For a moment I wondered if he was knocked out. But then....

"Ohhhhh...."

"Link, are you hurt?" Mom rushed out the door. Dad followed her.

"Ohhhhh...." Link sat up, obviously a little dizzy, and held his head.

"Don't move." That was a Mom thing she always said.

"Ohhhh...what happened?" He looked around. Then he saw my backpack at his feet. "Annie! You idiot! I'm going to strangle you! You about killed me with your stupid backpack." He started for me, limping somewhat. I ran back into the kitchen through the side door into the dining room and around back to the front hall, running up the stairs to my room.

"I'm gonna get you, Annie!"

I locked my door. I was safe, for a few moments, anyway.

Pick up your room—it's a mess. Mom's words echoed in my head. I looked around. Two pairs of jeans, two sweatshirts, underwear, and socks were on the floor. Magazine clippings from a history project were in one corner. A wet towel hung on the knob of my balcony door. In another corner I had been sorting old letters and photos in stacks. My room was not a mess. It just needed a little sweeping. I grabbed the towel and put the clothing into it. The paper stuff I swept under the blue throw rug. I looked at the room. Clean. Not bad for thirty seconds.

I flopped down crosswise on my bed facing the hallway door. *God, why does everyone in my family hate me? I don't do anything right. Mom and Dad yell at me. Link thinks I'm a pest. No one has any time for me at all unless it's to tell me to do something. Why can't I have a normal family?*

I rolled completely over on my bed. As I did I noticed an envelope on my pillow. I knew the handwriting right away—Grandma Rose's. I opened it.

Anne Rose Dear,

I sense a tumbling, troubled heart. A lot in life is like that. Hard times are inevitable. People will let you down. Some day I'll be gone. But God will always be there for you. Memorize this: "He will be the sure foundation for your times, a rich store of salvation and wisdom and knowledge; the fear of the LORD is the key to this treasure (Isaiah 33:6).

Loving you,
Grandma Rose

I read it three times. The third time things were a little blurry. I wiped the drop on the note, but the ink smeared a little. Grandma Rose always knew how to come through at the right time.

The whole God thing was pretty new to me still. I'd only come to know Him a week or so ago. He had been there for me when I felt I didn't have a friend in the world, and when I asked Him into my heart and said I'd trust Him, He showed me that I did have two great friends—Maria and Alia.

A sure foundation. *You're going to have to be my foundation, God. Things at home seem kind of messy right now. I'm not sure who I can depend on. But if Grandma Rose says You will always always be there for me, she must be right. She's been around a lot longer than I have.*

I stared at the card. The fear of the Lord is the key to this treasure. What was the treasure? God? *Will I ever be able to figure out my family? Will things ever fall into place, God? Maybe not? Well, I guess I'll just have to keep seeking You out. Everyone else around here is a little questionable. It seems only You are the Reliable One. So, I guess I'll just have to learn more about trusting You.*

I rolled over, looking up at the ceiling. There was the ceiling ladder handle, hanging down. It had started this whole mess. I breathed in deeply and exhaled slowly. *Annie,* I told myself, *just forget this trunk thing, just like Dad told you.*

"Annie!" It was Mom calling. "Dinner's ready."

I swung my legs over and jumped off the bed. But as I did, a small board from the wooden flooring popped up. Just what I needed—something else to break in my room. I bent down to fit it back into place. *Dumb house, with everything falling apart.*

But as I knelt down, I noticed that there seemed to be a small compartment below the floor where the board had been. I peered into the small hole. A small, old wooden box was in the hole. I lifted it out. It was small enough to fit into the palms of my two hands—a plain, hinged box with no exterior design.

I sat down on the floor. My heart was pounding. Had I discovered another of Sarah Millerton's secrets? I opened the box. Inside there was just one thing—a small, dark red velvet bag, pulled closed with a drawstring. It appeared empty, but as I felt it, there was one thing. Was it?…

I took a deep breath and pulled it open. I put my thumb and forefinger into the bag and drew out…A KEY! It was an old key with a three-hole design on the holding end and simple cuttings on the keyhole end.

I held it to my chest. The key to the treasure—just as Grandma Rose's Bible verse had said. As I held it, I knew: It was the key to my trunk!

23

MEETING SARAH

It was hard, but I kept the key a secret from my family. We'd had enough go-arounds about the trunk that I figured my showing them a key would make things worse. Since I was grounded from youth night at church and everything else, including the phone, I couldn't call Maria and Alia about it, either. When I showed them the velvet bag and key the next day, they about freaked. They had the same feeling as I—that it would open the trunk. The minutes barely crept along until three o'clock when the final bell rang. Grandma Rose was waiting at the front curb in her '57 Chevy.

We started the drive up to Western Mountain Hospital. It was my second time there. Just a week ago I sat on a bench near the adjacent rose garden and called out to God. I had told Him about my loneliness and asked Him to be my One True Friend. Since that prayer He had been helping me chill out a little and learn to be a friend to have friends.

I smiled at Maria and Alia as they got out of the backseat of Grandma Rose's car.

"What's with you?" asked Maria.

"Oh, nothing," I said. "I just like this place, okay?"

"You like hospitals?" asked Alia. "That's sick."

Grandma Rose dropped her keys into her rose-printed handbag. "Who's sick? You, Annie? Well, we've come to the right place."

I shook my head. Grandma Rose's hearing was a little off lately. I figured it wasn't worth explaining.

The red brick hospital was smaller than our middle school. It was sort of H-shaped, with an extra T-shaped wing for the convalescent patients.

We strolled through the main entrance and down the corridor of regular hospital rooms to the T wing. I could tell when one had changed to the other when I saw the lineup of wheelchairs. Old folks lined the hallway outside their rooms, watching the nursing world go by.

"Good afternoon, Myrtle." Grandma Rose patted the hand of one lady who didn't respond except for a nod and somewhat dazed look. "How are you, Carl?" She stopped at each chair and peeked into each room. She knew everyone—patients, nurses, even the blood technician who was pushing his little cart of vials down the hallway.

Grandma Rose stopped outside a room about halfway down the hallway. "Girls, this is Sarah's room. Now, she's a lovely lady, but she may say some confusing things because of her Alzheimer's disease."

"Like?" I asked.

"Well, she's in a stage of the disease where she forgets something from yesterday but can still recall things from many years ago. But some of that she's mixing up now, too." Grandma Rose looked at us and sighed. "You'll just need to…what would you say? Tune in? You may not get all your answers today."

Maria, Alia, and I followed Grandma Rose into Sarah's room. It was smaller than my bedroom, with two hospital beds, a large dresser, and nightstands. A frail, white-haired woman in a plain turquoise jogging suit was sitting in an overstuffed chair.

"Hello, Sarah." Grandma Rose placed her hand on Sarah's shoulder. "You look chipper today."

She didn't, really, though. She was somewhat hunched over and had been staring out the window. She turned slowly and looked at us. "Who are you? Are you the hairdresser? Where is your comb? How can you fix my hair if you don't have a comb?"

I looked at this woman. Though wispy, her hair was neatly in place. Obviously someone had fixed her hair that day.

"No, Sarah, I'm not the hairdresser. I'm Rose. Remember? I come to read you the Bible. We're reading through Isaiah now." Grandma Rose smiled at me. So that's why she had jotted down that Bible verse for me.

Sarah stared out the window again for a moment. Outside the rose garden was turning brown in the cool autumn air. Then she turned and smiled at Grandma Rose, her eyes suddenly sparkling. "The grass withers and the flowers fall, but the word of our God stands forever."

"That's right, Sarah: Isaiah 40:8." Grandma Rose turned toward us. "I brought you some visitors." She motioned us over toward Sarah. "This is my granddaughter, Annie, and her friends, Maria and Alia."

Sarah looked us over, with a puzzled expression on her face at first, then her eyes began to water. "Anne?"

I nodded and smiled, holding out my hand.

She took it and pulled me gently closer. "Oh, my Anne Leah. Why haven't you visited me sooner? I've missed you so."

"But I…I'm.…"

"And your brother, Charles. He hasn't come to see me, either. It's a shameful thing when children run off and leave their parents to live all alone." Suddenly she stopped talking and stared out the window again.

I looked at Grandma Rose. She put her finger to her lips. She pulled over a desk chair next to Sarah and sat down, then motioned for us to sit on her bed.

"Sarah, this isn't your Anne Leah. This is my granddaughter, Annie. Your Anne went away a long time ago, remember? And Charles too?"

Sarah turned toward Grandma Rose. Tears were finding their way, one by one, down the crevices in her worn face. Grandma Rose pulled a Kleenex out of her coat pocket and patted Sarah's face gently. Sarah took the Kleenex from her and wiped her own eyes. Her eyes then went from vacant to bright again.

"I'm a silly old lady, aren't I?" Sarah sighed. "Well, if you're not going to fix my hair, let's have some tea."

Grandma Rose said she'd round some up and stepped out

of the room, leaving us alone with Sarah.

I looked around the circumference of the room, swinging my feet in the chair and wondering how to end the silence.

"So, do you girls know my Charles?" We shook our heads. "He never comes, you know. But it's not his fault. You see, I gave him up—many years ago. I gave him up. I gave up my own son." She looked at us, and her look went through us. Pain had etched her face for many years. And pain was still at work.

Alia reached over and took Sarah's wrinkled hand in her two smooth ones. "Sarah, God understands. He gave up His son, too. He gave His Son Jesus so we could have life. I bet that was the hardest thing He ever did. But now we have life because of God's gift." Alia caressed Sarah's hand gently. I stared at my friend in awe. Sometimes Alia amazed me. Most times she seemed like such a ditz, but at other times—the hardest times—she just knew exactly what to say.

Sarah's expression softened. "I always wanted to go to Placerton to see him. It's just down the road a piece. Those folks were so nice, taking in my baby. I just pray that the Wellcorns have taken good care of my little boy."

Grandma Rose stood in the doorway with a red plastic tray. On it were teacups and saucers, a stainless pitcher with steaming water, and paper towels. "This is not exactly elegant, but I think it'll hit the spot."

But I wasn't paying much attention to the instant tea party makings. Wellcorns. That name rung a bell somewhere. An odd name. *You'd think I'd be able to place a face with a name like that. God, send something fast on the Internet. My own database is a blank.*

24

NO COINCIDENCE

Grandma Rose had an appointment to take Shakespeare to the vet, so we parted ways at the hospital. I was itching to go back to the newspaper and museum to find out some information about the Wellcorns. If Sarah were right, the heir to the trunk might be right in the town just eleven miles up the road.

"But what if he doesn't want to be found?" said Alia. "Maybe he wouldn't want to meet his real mother."

"And what if we do find the trunk—you'd just give the lost Mountain Center fortune away to someone you just met?" Maria stood there outside the hospital with her hands on her hips.

"I don't know," I said. "Something just happened to me there in the hospital with Sarah. She seems so sad. If we could find her son.... Oh, I don't know. Let's just see what we can find out."

We walked a half dozen blocks to the downtown area and then shortcut through an alley on our way to the museum.

"I don't like alleys," said Alia, straggling behind and looking over her shoulder. "You could run into something weird."

"Like what?" Maria was setting a confident pace. "A kidnapper or something?"

"Yeah," said Alia. "Or a cat bugle."

"Burglar," Maria corrected.

I stopped. A pickup truck was parked down the alley a few stores ahead at the back entrance to Mountain Center Antiques, blocking the way. It was a shiny, new black truck, with a half load of firewood toward the front of the bed. But at the rear of the bed something caught my eye. "Not a cat burglar, Alia. But maybe a trunk burglar."

Maria and Alia froze behind me. They had seen, just as I had, a man standing on the bed of the truck and pushing a trunk toward the tailgate. An old trunk. *My* trunk!

Part of me wanted to turn and run. A man who would steal something out of someone's home could be shady enough to hurt us if we confronted him. But most of me wanted to throttle him! This man had stolen my trunk! No, he had stolen *Sarah's* trunk. He had stolen a part of a sweet old woman's life. And I was going to get it back.

"Hey, you!"

The man, who was now lifting the trunk off the tailgate, turned around and noticed us just a store away from him. He was wearing black jeans and a black leather jacket. His hair was cut short and slicked back.

"What are you doing? That's my trunk you've got there!" I stood as tall as I could. But beneath my squared-off shoulders my knees were shaking.

He set it down, and I knew he was glaring at me through his dark sunglasses. "Get lost! This trunk is mine. And you're not going to take it away." He picked up the trunk and started to lift it back onto the pickup bed.

I looked at Maria and Alia and gave them the one–two–three cue with my fingers. Together we screamed, "Help!" The man set the trunk back down again and reached instead for a broom that was lying in the truck. He turned toward us with it. We stepped back and continued to scream, and just then the back door of the antique store opened and the owner, George Harris, stepped out dressed in a blue nylon jogging suit.

"What's going...."

I stepped toward him, pointing at the man with the trunk. "He's got my trunk, sir. He was bringing it to your store, but it's my trunk. Remember? You saw it at my house the other day."

He pulled back his baseball cap and scratched his dark hair. "Kind of looks like your trunk. In fact, yes, it is. I remember that lock." He looked up at the man. "Did you take this girl's trunk?"

He scowled. "It's mine. They cheated me out of it. They knew it was in the house when they bought it and didn't tell me."

I inched toward the trunk. "So you are Edward Tristan— Sarah Millerton's former trustee?"

"Right, Sherlocks," he said sarcastically. "I handled her affairs. Until I lost my license to practice law, that is." He laughed, seemingly to himself. "And I never got what I should have. The old lady was supposed to be loaded. As it turns out, the house was just full of old junk. There was a rumor about a trunk filled with gold. But I never found it."

"So when you heard about a trunk, you thought you could just come and steal it?" I was gritting my teeth.

"That's right, little girl. The Reel lady told me about it. So when I got into town, I went straight to the house. The lights were all turned off except in the entry hall. No one was in sight. And there was the trunk, right at the foot of the stairs."

"So you just walked in our house and took it? How could you do that?" The guy was making me mad!

He nodded and grinned a thin little smirk. "Easy, Sherlocks. The door was open. No one was around. I picked it up. I left. I was only taking what was mine."

George Harris stepped toward him. "Well, you can explain that to the judge. Girls, run in the shop and call 911. I'll just make sure he doesn't…."

But as we started toward the back door of the shop, the man shouted, "You don't know who you're dealing with, you small town jerks. Just try and stop me."

Then he ran to his truck, started the engine and gunned it down the alley. We started running after him, but the locksmith waved us down. "Call the police!" he yelled, and then he himself started down the alley toward his own truck, parked next to the building. But just at that moment, the getaway truck hit a pothole as it approached the intersection and the heavy suspension of the truck made it bounce, bounce, bounce for a few feet. The trunk bounced, bounced, bounced too, and then fell off the back of the truck as it careened around the corner.

"Look!" I started running. The others did too. George Harris was the first there, and he righted the trunk and looked it over. It had some scrapes from the rough landing, but it was still intact.

"I think it'll be okay," he said, brushing off some gravel dust. "Here, I'll carry it back to the shop for you. It'll be safe there, and we can call the sheriff's office. They'll catch that guy." He smiled. Suddenly he didn't look like someone who wanted to take my treasure but more like an angel in a jogging suit and tennies.

I nodded from relief and collapsed into my two friends' waiting arms in a group hug.

Maria suddenly stood back and held me by the shoulders. "Annie! The key! You've got the key! Let's go try it right now."

I reached into my right jacket pocket and felt for the velvet bag. I pulled it out and the three of us hurried to the back door of the antique shop. Inside the locksmith was setting the trunk down in his back workroom. He headed for a corner work desk where he sat and picked up the phone.

Probably dialing 911, I thought. I pulled the key out of the bag and looked at it a moment. Then I looked at Maria and Alia. *Go on*, their eyes pleaded.

I knelt down in front of the trunk and fit the key into the lock. Then I turned it. The lock gave way to the key and the latch flipped forward. I breathed in deeply.

"C'mon," said Maria. "I can't stand it."

"Guys, whatever is inside belongs to Sarah." I looked at my friends for agreement. "Right?"

Maria looked crestfallen for a second, but when she saw Alia nodding, she did too. I lifted the lid. I immediately noticed a musty pungency. Whatever was in there had been there a long time. I held my breath as I lifted the old packaging paper that lay on top. And then I let it all out. Underneath were two stacks of clothing...and blankets. Baby stuff.

I carefully lifted the items, one by one, handing them alternately to Maria, then Alia, who peered over my shoulder. Baby gowns. A blanket. Carefully embroidered square cloths—old-time diapers, probably.

At the bottom was an old round box with a lid. It had a pretty pink floral paper covering on it.

George Harris walked over to watch. "Found the key, huh? Hmmm, that's an old hat box."

I looked at it. Maybe Sarah had hidden the lost Mountain Center fortune in that box. I lifted the lid. Inside was a long satin baby gown, with pretty smocking and carefully stitched edges. With it was a matching cap.

Suddenly my eyes watered. All of those baby things were meant for Anne Leah, Sarah's daughter who had died at birth. She had probably spent months of her waiting time rocking in that chair we found in the attic and making each of those sweet little things. How sad it must have been to give birth to a little girl who would never see her mama's eyes and smile.

I put the gown and cap back into the box. "They're Sarah's little baby girl's things." I tried to blink away the wetness, but it streamed down instead.

"That gown was probably for her christening," Maria said.

"Christening?" I reached for the things my friends were holding and started putting them away too.

"Babies are christened in my church," Maria said. "You know, like baptism."

"Oh."

We stood there a moment in silence. Those little clothes and blankets represented a sad chapter of a woman's life. As I thought about it, I felt all mixed up and yucky inside. All that time I'd hoped we would discover some big pile of money—a fortune. Instead we had opened up a trunk of someone else's memories.

"Guys, there's one thing that confuses me. If her baby girl died at birth and her husband was gone, why did Sarah give up the other baby?"

Maria and Alia slowly raised their shoulders and shook their heads. Then Maria said, "Maybe her family made her do it."

"Or maybe she just wanted Charles to have a better life," said Alia. "So she gave him to the Wellcorns."

Wellcorns. What was it about that name? I knew I'd heard it before. But I really didn't know that many people in Mountain Center. Still, it sounded so famil....Suddenly I had it!

"Girls, come with me. We have one more stop to make."

25

FAMILY

"Annie, I said what are we doing here?" Maria did not like being dragged.

"It is getting a little late, Annie." Alia was two steps behind again. "I've got homework."

"I've just got to check one more thing to close this case." I pulled the door open at the Mountain Center Museum.

Docent Dora was on duty again. "W-w-welcome to the Mountain Center...."

"Uh, thanks, Dora," I interrupted, "but I'm looking for...."

"Can I help you?" From behind the front counter walked Grandma Rose's friend with his name tag that read: JOHN CORNWALL. Not Well-corn. Corn-wall.

"Hi, Mr. Cornwall," I said. "Can we talk to you a minute?" I motioned to a table in a corner of the front room. He politely pulled each of our chairs out a little, and we all sat down.

"I'm going to get right to it, Mr. Cornwall." I leaned on the table to steady my nerves. "Were you raised in Placerton?"

"Why, yes."

"And were you adopted?"

"Well, Dear Abby would probably say that's a personal question, but yes, I was."

"And…and is your birthday July 23, 1921?"

"My goodness, how do you know that?"

I sighed. "Mr. Cornwall, boy, do I have a story to tell you."

It didn't take long to tell him about what we'd learned about Sarah Millerton and her life. John Cornwall then called his adoptive mother's sister—who was still alive and confirmed the story she'd kept secret all those years. John Cornwall was Sarah Millerton's son, Charles. We were so excited that we called Grandma Rose. After another few phone calls, we all arranged to meet at the hospital that night for a visit with Sarah.

Grandma Rose picked us up, and we met John Cornwall at the hospital right after dinner. By then I could tell them that the locksmith had called, and the sheriff had caught the man in the pickup truck. Edward Tristan, the former trustee, had been wanted in suspicion of stealing from other old folks' estates too. Esther Reel had been an innocent pawn used by Tristan.

And I also told them that, yes, there was a small headstone behind the trees that bordered our backyard. All it said was "BABY GIRL" on it.

Outside Sarah's room, I bit my nails. "Grandma Rose, Mr.

Cornwall, do you think we're doing the right thing?"

John Cornwall put his hand on my shoulder. "Annie, my adoptive parents have been gone a long time. Sarah has no family. She probably needs me, and I need her." He smiled.

Grandma Rose led us in. "Sarah? Sarah, you have some visitors."

Sarah sat with some knitting in her window chair. She looked up, confused.

Grandma Rose took her hand. "This is my granddaughter, Annie, and her friends, Maria and Alia. Remember? They visited you earlier today."

Sarah nodded, but it was clear that she didn't remember us.

"And this is John Cornwall, the son of the Cornwalls in Placerton," Grandma Rose said, gesturing to John Cornwall. "Sarah, this is your son, Charles. We—that is, Annie and her friends—found him for you."

Sarah still looked confused for a moment, and then all at once her big wall of sadness fell, and she held her frail arms out toward him. John Cornwall, dabbing his eyes with a handkerchief, slowly got down on his knees and put his arms around his mother and held her. They rocked each other for many long moments as the rest of us looked on.

Seeing her son opened a whole floodgate for Sarah. She told us all how his father was a gold miner and had had a dispute with Sarah's family over a gold claim. They were married secretly and were about to tell her family when her husband mysteriously disappeared. Her family nearly disowned her when they learned of the marriage, and so,

Sarah, gave up the baby to try and make peace.

As I watched Sarah and John Cornwall sit together, holding hands, I knew I was right. After all the years and all the pain, these two still loved each other. Maybe, just maybe, my family and I would also get beyond our misunderstandings and arguments. I was beginning to learn that God could help.

As we left, I had another idea. "Mr. Cornwall, I was thinking that my trunk—I mean Sarah's trunk—would make a great addition to your nursery room at the museum. And the rocking chair and the cradle, too. I think Mom will agree."

His eyes lit up. "Annie, that's a wonderful idea. Seeing the things might make my mother sad, but at the museum they could give a lot of other people joy."

He held open the outside door. "And I had an idea, too. It's still a mystery about what happened to my father, Albert Millerton. Think you could check that one out? Are you sleuths still in business after all this?"

I looked at Maria and Alia. Their eyes brightened, and we all nodded our heads. "I've got a story to write for the newspaper, but sure!"

"Well, fine," he said, taking Grandma Rose's arm. "And by the way, please call me John. I think we're going to become good friends."

I sighed as I watched him lead Grandma Rose to her car. But I had to admit it: It was *not* a coincidence that John Cornwall came into our lives. It was a God thing. I sighed again. My family sure was changing. But instead of losing a grandma,